THE ONLY STORY

Center Point
Large Print

Also by Julian Barnes and available from Center Point Large Print:

Levels of Life

**This Large Print Book carries the
Seal of Approval of N.A.V.H.**

THE
ONLY
STORY

JULIAN BARNES

CENTER POINT LARGE PRINT
THORNDIKE, MAINE

This Center Point Large Print edition is published in the year 2018 by arrangement with Alfred A. Knopf, an imprint of The Knopf Doubleday Publishing Group, a division of Penguin Random House, LLC.

The text of this Large Print edition is unabridged. In other aspects, this book may vary from the original edition. Printed in the United States of America on permanent paper. Set in 16-point Times New Roman type.

ISBN: 978-1-68324-837-8

Library of Congress Cataloging-in-Publication Data

Names: Barnes, Julian, author.
Title: The only story / Julian Barnes.
Description: Center Point Large Print edition. | Thorndike, Maine : Center Point Large Print, 2018.
Identifiers: LCCN 2018013808 | ISBN 9781683248378 (hardcover : alk. paper)
Subjects: LCSH: Man-woman relationships—Fiction. | Psychological fiction. | Large type books. | BISAC: FICTION / Literary. | FICTION / Coming of Age. | FICTION / Psychological. | GSAFD: Bildungsromans.
Classification: LCC PR6052.A6657 O55 2018b | DDC 823/.914—dc23
LC record available at https://lccn.loc.gov/2018013808

to Hermione

Novel: A small tale, generally of love.

—Samuel Johnson, *A Dictionary of the English Language* (1755)

THE ONLY STORY

ONE

Would you rather love the more, and suffer the more; or love the less, and suffer the less? That is, I think, finally, the only real question.

You may point out—correctly—that it isn't a real question. Because we don't have the choice. If we had the choice, then there would be a question. But we don't, so there isn't. Who can control how much they love? If you can control it, then it isn't love. I don't know what you call it instead, but it isn't love.

Most of us have only one story to tell. I don't mean that only one thing happens to us in our lives: there are countless events, which we turn into countless stories. But there's only one that matters, only one finally worth telling. This is mine.

But here's the first problem. If this is your only story, then it's the one you have most often told and retold, even if—as is the case here—mainly to yourself. The question then is: Do all these retellings bring you closer to the truth of what happened, or move you further away? I'm not sure. One test might be whether, as the years pass, you come out better from your own story, or worse. To come out worse might indicate that you are being more truthful. On the other hand, there is the danger of being retrospectively anti-heroic: making yourself out to have behaved worse than you actually did can be a form of self-praise. So I shall have to be careful. Well, I have learned to become careful over the years. As careful now as I was careless then. Or do I mean carefree? Can a word have two opposites?

The time, the place, the social milieu? I'm not sure how important they are in stories about love. Perhaps in the old days, in the classics, where there are battles between love and duty, love and religion, love and family, love and the state. This isn't one of those stories. But still, if you insist. The time: more than fifty years ago. The place: about fifteen miles south of London. The milieu: stockbroker belt, as they called it—not that I ever met a stockbroker in all my years there. Detached houses, some half-timbered, some tile-hung. Hedges of privet, laurel and beech. Roads with gutters as yet unencumbered by yellow lines and residents' parking bays. This was a time when you could drive up to London and park almost anywhere. Our particular zone of suburban sprawl was cutely known as "The Village," and decades previously it might possibly have counted as one. Now it contained

12

a station from which suited men went up to London Monday to Friday, and some for an extra half-day on Saturday. There was a Green Line bus stop; a zebra crossing with Belisha beacons; a post office; a church unoriginally named after St. Michael; a pub, a general store, chemist, hairdresser; a petrol station which did elementary car repairs. In the mornings, you heard the electric whine of milk floats—choose between Express and United Dairies; in the evenings, and at weekends (though never on a Sunday morning) the chug of petrol-driven lawnmowers.

Vocal, incompetent cricket was played on the Village green; there was a golf course and a tennis club. The soil was sandy enough to please gardeners; London clay didn't reach this far out. Recently, a delicatessen had opened, which some thought subversive in its offerings of European goods: smoked cheeses, and knobbly sausages hanging like donkey cocks in their string webbing. But the Village's younger wives were beginning to cook more adventurously, and their husbands mainly approved. Of the two available TV channels, BBC was watched more than ITV, while alcohol was generally drunk only at weekends. The chemist would sell verruca plasters and dry shampoo in little puffer bottles, but not contraceptives; the general store sold the narcoleptic local *Advertiser & Gazette*, but not even the mildest girlie mag. For sexual items, you had to travel up to London. None of this bothered me for most of my time there.

Right, that's my estate agent's duties concluded (there was a real one ten miles away). And one other thing: don't ask me about the weather. I don't much remember what the weather has been like during my life. True, I can remember how hot sun gave greater impetus to sex; how sudden snow delighted, and how cold, damp days set off those early symptoms that eventually led to a double hip replacement. But nothing significant in my life ever happened during, let alone because of, weather. So if you don't mind, meteorology will play no part in my story. Though you are free to deduce, when I am found playing grass-court tennis, that it was neither raining nor snowing at the time.

The tennis club: Who would have thought it might begin there? Growing up, I regarded the place as merely an outdoor branch of the Young Conservatives. I owned a racket and had played a bit, just as I could bowl a few useful overs of off-spin, and turn out as a goalkeeper of solid yet occasionally reckless temperament. I was competitive at sport without being unduly talented.

At the end of my first year at university, I was at home for three months, visibly and unrepentantly bored. Those of the same age today will find it hard to imagine the laboriousness of communication back then. Most of my friends were far-flung, and—by some unexpressed but clear parental mandate—use of the telephone was discouraged. A letter, and then a letter in reply. It was all slow-paced, and lonely.

My mother, perhaps hoping that I would meet a nice blond Christine, or a sparky, black-ringleted Virginia—in either case, one of reliable, if not too pronounced, Conservative tendencies— suggested that I might like to join the tennis club. She would even sub me for it. I laughed silently at the motivation: the one thing I was not going to do with my existence was end up in suburbia with a tennis wife and 2.4 children, and watch them in turn find their mates at the club, and so on, down some echoing enfilade of mirrors, into an endless, privet-and-laurel future. When I accepted my mother's offer, it was in a spirit of nothing but satire.

I went along, and was invited to "play in." This was a test in which not just my tennis game but my general deportment and social suitability would be quietly examined in a decorous English way. If I failed to display negatives, then positives would be assumed: this was how it worked. My mother had ensured that my whites were laundered, and the creases in my shorts both evident and parallel; I reminded myself not to swear, burp or fart on court. My game was wristy, optimistic and largely self-taught; I played as they would have expected me to play, leaving out the shit-shots I most enjoyed, and never hitting straight at an opponent's body. Serve, in to the net, volley, second volley, drop shot, lob, while quick to show appreciation of the opponent—"Too good!"—and proper concern for the partner—"Mine!" I was modest after a good shot, quietly pleased at the winning of a game, head-shakingly rueful at the ultimate loss of a set. I could feign all that stuff, and so was welcomed as a summer member, joining the year-round Hugos and Carolines.

The Hugos liked to tell me that I had raised the club's average IQ while lowering its average age; one insisted on calling me Clever Clogs and Herr Professor in deft allusion to my having completed one year at Sussex University. The Carolines were friendly enough, but wary; they knew better where they stood with the Hugos. When I was among this tribe, I felt my natural competitiveness leach away. I tried to play my best shots, but winning didn't engage me. I even used to practise reverse cheating. If a ball fell a couple of inches out, I would give a running thumbs up to the opponent, and a shout of "Too good!" Similarly, a serve pushed an inch or so too long or too wide would produce a slow nod

16

of assent, and a trudge across to receive the next serve. "Decent cove, that Paul fellow," I once overheard a Hugo admit to another Hugo. When shaking hands after a defeat, I would deliberately praise some aspect of their game. "That kicker of a serve to the backhand—gave me a lot of trouble," I would candidly admit. I was only there for a couple of months, and did not want them to know me.

After three weeks or so of my temporary membership, there was a Lucky Dip Mixed Doubles tournament. The pairings were drawn by lot. Later, I remember thinking: Lot is another name for destiny, isn't it? I was paired with Mrs. Susan Macleod, who was clearly not a Caroline. She was, I guessed, somewhere in her forties, with her hair pulled back by a ribbon, revealing her ears, which I failed to notice at the time. A white tennis dress with green trim, and a line of green buttons down the front of the bodice. She was almost exactly my height, which is five feet nine if I am lying and adding an inch.

"Which side do you prefer?" she asked.

"Side?"

"Forehand or backhand?"

"Sorry. I don't really mind."

"You take the forehand to begin with, then."

Our first match—the format was single-set knockout—was against one of the thicker Hugos and dumpier Carolines. I scampered around a lot, thinking it my job to take more of the balls; and at first, when at the net, would do a quarter-turn to see how my partner was coping, and if and how the ball was coming back. But it always did come back, with smoothly hit groundstrokes, so I stopped turning, relaxed, and found myself really, really wanting to win. Which we did, 6–2.

As we sat with glasses of lemon barley water, I said,

"Thanks for saving my arse."

I was referring to the number of times I had lurched across the net in order to intercept, only to miss the ball and put Mrs. Macleod off.

"The phrase is, 'Well played, partner.' " Her eyes were grey-blue, her smile steady. "And try serving from a bit wider. It opens up the angles."

I nodded, accepting the advice while feeling no jab to my ego, as I would if it had come from a Hugo.

"Anything else?"

"The most vulnerable spot in doubles is always down the middle."

"Thanks, Mrs. Macleod."

"Susan."

"I'm glad you're not a Caroline," I found myself saying.

She chuckled, as if she knew exactly what I meant. But how could she have?

"Does your husband play?"

"My husband? Mr. E.P.?" She laughed. "No. Golf's his game. I think it's plain unsporting to hit a stationary ball. Don't you agree?"

There was too much in this answer for me to unpack at once, so I just gave a nod and a quiet grunt.

The second match was harder, against a couple who kept breaking off to have quiet tactical conversations, as if preparing for marriage. At one point, when Mrs. Macleod was serving, I tried the cheap ploy of crouching below the level of the net almost on the centre line, aiming to distract the returner. It worked for a couple of points, but then, at 30–15, I rose too quickly on hearing the thwock of the serve and the ball hit me square in the back of the head. I keeled over melodramatically and rolled into the bottom of the net. Caroline and Hugo raced forward in a show of concern while from behind me came only a riot of laughter, and a girlish "Shall we play a let?," which our opponents naturally disputed. Still, we squeaked the set 7–5, and were into the quarter-finals.

"Trouble up next," she warned me. "County level. On their way down now, but no free gifts."

And there weren't any. We were well beaten, for all my intense scurrying. When I tried to protect us down the middle, the ball went wide; when I covered the angles, it was thumped down the centre line. The two games we got were as much as we deserved.

We sat on a bench and fed our rackets into their presses. Mine was a Dunlop Maxply; hers a Gray's.

"I'm sorry I let you down," I said.

"No one let anyone down."

"I think my problem may be that I'm tactically naive."

Yes, it was a bit pompous, but even so I was surprised by her giggles.

"You're a case," she said. "I'm going to have to call you Casey."

I smiled. I liked the idea of being a case.

As we went our separate ways to shower, I said, "Would you like a lift? I've got a car."

She looked at me sideways. "Well, I wouldn't want a lift if you haven't got a car. That would be counterproductive." There was something in the way she said it that made it impossible to take offence. "But what about your reputation?"

"My reputation?" I answered. "I don't think I've got one."

"Oh dear. We'll have to get you one then. Every young man should have a reputation."

Writing all this down, it seems more knowing than it was at the time. And "nothing happened." I drove Mrs. Macleod to her house in Duckers Lane, she got out, I went home, and gave an abbreviated account of the afternoon to my

20

parents. Lucky Dip Mixed Doubles. Partners chosen by lot.

"Quarter-finals, Paul," said my mother. "I'd have come along and watched if I'd known."

I realised that this was probably the last thing in the history of the world that I wanted, or would ever want.

Perhaps you've understood a little too quickly; I can hardly blame you. We tend to slot any new relationship we come across into a preexisting category. We see what is general or common about it; whereas the participants see—feel—only what is individual and particular to them. We say: how predictable; they say: what a surprise! One of the things I thought about Susan and me—at the time, and now, again, all these years later—is that there often didn't seem *words* for our relationship; at least, none that fitted. But perhaps this is an illusion all lovers have about themselves: that they escape both category and description.

My mother, of course, was never stuck for a phrase.

As I said, I drove Mrs. Macleod home, and nothing happened. And again; and again. Except that this depends on what you mean by "nothing." Not a touch, not a kiss, not a word, let alone a scheme or a plan. But there was already, just in the way we sat in the car, before she said a few laughing words and then walked off up her driveway, a complicity between us. Not, I insist, as yet a complicity to *do* anything. Just a complicity which made me a little more me, and her a little more her.

Had there been any scheme or plan, we would have behaved differently. We might have met secretly, or disguised our intentions. But we were innocent; and so I was taken aback when my mother, over a supper of stultifying boredom, said to me,

"Operating a taxi service now, are we?"

I looked at her in bewilderment. It was always my mother who policed me. My father was milder, and less given to judgement. He preferred to allow things to blow over, to let sleeping dogs lie, not to stir up mud; whereas my mother preferred facing facts and not brushing things under the carpet. My parents' marriage, to my unforgiving nineteen-year-old eye, was a car crash of cliché. Though I would have to admit, as the one making the judgement, that a "car crash of cliché" is itself a cliché.

But I refused to be a cliché, at least this early in my life, and so I looked across at my mother with blank belligerence.

"Mrs. Macleod will be putting on weight, the amount you're ferrying her around" was my mother's unkindly elaboration of her original point.

"Not with all the tennis she plays," I answered casually.

"Mrs. Macleod," she went on. "What's her first name?"

"I don't actually know," I lied.

"Have you come across the Macleods, Andy?"

"There's a Macleod at the golf club," he answered. "Short, fat guy. Hits the ball as if he hates it."

"Maybe we should ask them round for sherry."

As I winced at the prospect, my father replied, "There isn't enough call for that, is there?"

"Anyway," continued my mother, tenacious of subject, "I thought she had a bicycle."

"You suddenly seem to know a lot about her," I replied.

"Don't you start getting pert with me, Paul." Her colour was rising.

"Leave The Lad alone, Bets," said my father quietly.

"It's not *me* who should be leaving him alone."

"Please may I get down now, Mummy?" I asked with an eight-year-old's whine. Well, if they were going to treat me like a child . . .

"Maybe we *should* ask them round for sherry." I couldn't tell if my father was being dense, or whimsically ironic.

"Don't *you* start as well," my mother said sharply. "He doesn't get it from me."

I went to the tennis club the next afternoon, and the next. As I started hacking away with two Carolines and a Hugo I noticed Susan in play on the court beyond. It was fine while I had my back to her game. But when I looked past my opponents and saw her rocking gently sideways on the balls of her feet as she prepared to receive serve, I lost immediate interest in the next point.

Later, I offer her a lift.

"Only if you've got a car."

I mumble something in reply.

"Whatski, Mr. Casey?"

We are facing one another. I feel at the same time baffled and at ease. She is wearing her usual tennis dress, and I find myself wondering if its green buttons undo, or are merely ornamental. I have never met anyone like her before. Our faces are at exactly the same height, nose to nose, mouth to mouth, ear to ear. She is clearly noticing the same.

"If I were wearing heels, I could see over the net," she says. "As it is, we're seeing eye to eye."

I can't work out if she is confident or nervous; if she is always like this, or just with me. Her words look flirty, but didn't feel so at the time.

I have put the top of my Morris Minor convertible down. If I am operating a bloody taxi service, then I don't see why the bloody Village shouldn't see who the bloody passengers are. Or rather, who the passenger is.

"By the way," I say, as I slow and put the car into second. "My parents might be asking you and your husband round for sherry."

"Lordy-Lordy," she replies, putting her hand in front of her mouth. "But I never take Mr. Elephant Pants anywhere."

"Why do you call him that?"

"It just came to me one day. I was hanging up his clothes and he's got these grey flannel trousers, several pairs of them, with an eighty-four-inch waistline, and I held up one pair and thought to myself, that looks just like the back half of a pantomime elephant."

"My dad says he hits a golf ball as if he hates it."

"Yes, well. What else do they say?"

"My mother says you'll be getting fat, what with all the lifts I'm giving you."

She doesn't reply. I stop the car at the end of her driveway and look across. She is anxious, almost solemn.

"Sometimes I forget about other people. About them existing. People I've never met, I mean. I'm sorry, Casey, maybe I should have . . . I mean, it isn't as if . . . oh dear."

"Nonsense," I say firmly. "You said a young man like me should have a reputation. It seems I've now got a reputation for operating a taxi service. That'll do me for the summer."

25

She remains downcast. Then says quietly, "Oh Casey, don't give up on me just yet."

But why would I, when I was falling smack into love?

So what words might you reach for, nowadays, to describe a relationship between a nineteen-year-old boy, or nearly-man, and a forty-eight-year-old woman? Perhaps those tabloid terms "cougar" and "toy boy"? But such words weren't around then, even if people behaved like that in advance of their naming. Or you might think: French novels, older woman teaching "the arts of love" to younger man, *ooh la la.* But there was nothing French about our relationship, or about us. We were English, and so had only those morally laden English words to deal with: words like scarlet woman, and adulteress. But there was never anyone less scarlet than Susan; and, as she once told me, when she first heard people talking about adultery, she thought it referred to the watering-down of milk.

Nowadays we talk about transactional sex, and recreational sex. No one, back then, had recreational sex. Well, they might have done, but they didn't call it that. Back then, back there, there was love, and there was sex, and there was a commingling of the two, sometimes awkward, sometimes seamless, which sometimes worked out, and sometimes didn't.

• • •

An exchange between my parents (read: my mother) and me, one of those English exchanges which condenses paragraphs of animosity into a pair of phrases.

"But I'm *nine-teen.*"

"*Exactly*—you're *only* nineteen."

We were each other's second lover: quasi-virgins, in effect. I had had my sexual induction—the usual bout of tender, anxious scuffle-and-blunder—with a girl at university, towards the end of my third term; while Susan, despite having two children and being married for a quarter of a century, was no more experienced than me. In retrospect, perhaps it would have been different if one of us had known more. But who, in love, looks forward to retrospect? And anyway, do I mean "more experienced in sex" or "more experienced in love"?

But I see I'm getting ahead of myself.

That first afternoon, when I had played in with my Dunlop Maxply and laundered whites, there was a huddle in the clubhouse over tea and cakes. The blazers were still assessing me for suitability, I realised. Checking that I was acceptably middle class, with all that this entailed. There was some joshing about the length of my hair, which was mostly contained by my headband. And almost as a follow-on to this I was asked what I thought about politics.

"I'm afraid I'm not remotely interested in politics," I replied.

"Well, that means you're a Conservative," said one committee member, and we all laughed.

When I tell her about this exchange, Susan nods and says, "I'm Labour, but it's a secret. Well, it was until now. So what do you make of that, my fine and feathered friend?"

I say that it doesn't bother me at all.

The first time I went to the Macleod house, Susan told me to come in the back way and walk up through the garden; I approved such informality. I pushed open an unlocked gate, then followed an unsteady brick path alongside compost heaps and bins of leaf mould; there was rhubarb growing up through a chimney pot, a quartet of raggedy fruit trees and a vegetable plot. A dishevelled old gardener was double-digging a square patch of earth. I nodded to him with the authority of a young academic approving a peasant. He nodded back.

As Susan was boiling the kettle, I looked around me. The house was similar to ours, except that everything felt a bit classier; or rather, here the old things looked inherited rather than bought secondhand. There were standard lamps with yellowing parchment shades. There was also—

not exactly a carelessness, more an insouciance about things not being orderly. I could see golf clubs in a bag lying in the hallway, and a couple of glasses still not cleared away from lunch— perhaps even the previous night. Nothing went uncleared-away in our house. Everything had to be tidied, washed, swept, polished, in case someone called round unexpectedly. But who might do so? The vicar? The local policeman? Someone wanting to make a phone call? A door-to-door salesman? The truth was that nobody ever arrived without invitation, and all that tidying and wiping was performed out of what struck me as deep social atavism. Whereas here, people like me called round and the place looked, as my mother would no doubt have observed, as if it hadn't seen a duster for a fortnight.

"Your gardener's jolly hardworking," I say, for want of a better conversational opener.

Susan looks at me and bursts out laughing. "Gardener? That's the Master of the Establishment, as it happens. His Lordship."

"I'm terribly sorry. Please don't tell him. I just thought . . ."

"Still, I'm glad he looks up to snuff. Like a real gardener. Old Adam. Precisely." She hands me a cup of tea. "Milk? Sugar?"

You understand, I hope, that I'm telling you everything as I remember it? I never kept a diary,

29

and most of the participants in my story—my story! my life!—are either dead or far dispersed. So I'm not necessarily putting it down in the order that it happened. I think there's a different authenticity to memory, and not an inferior one. Memory sorts and sifts according to the demands made on it by the rememberer. Do we have access to the algorithm of its priorities? Probably not. But I would guess that memory prioritises whatever is most useful to help keep the bearer of those memories going. So there would be a self-interest in bringing happier memories to the surface first. But again, I'm only guessing.

For instance, I remember lying in bed one night, being kept awake by one of those stomach-slapping erections which, when you are young, you carelessly—or carefreely—imagine will last you the rest of your life. But this one was different. You see, it was a kind of generalised erection, unconnected to any person, or dream, or fantasy. It was more about just being joyfully young. Young in brain, heart, cock, soul—and it just happened to be the cock which best articulated that general state.

It seems to me that when you are young, you think about sex most of the time, but you don't reflect on it much. You are so intent on the who, when, where, how—or rather, more often, the great if—that you think less about the why and the whither. Before you first have sex, you've heard all sorts of things about it; nowadays far more, and far earlier, and far more graphically, than when I was young. But it all amounts to the same input: a mixture of sentimentality, pornography and misrepresentation. When I look back at my youth, I see it as a time of cock-vigour so insistent that it forbade examination of what such vigour was for.

Perhaps I don't understand the young now. I'd like to talk to them and ask how things are for them and their friends—but then a shyness creeps in. And perhaps I didn't even understand the young when I was young. That could be true too.

But in case you're wondering, I don't envy the young. In my days of adolescent rage and insolence, I would ask myself: What are the old for, if not to envy the young? That seemed to me their principal and final purpose before extinction. I was walking to meet Susan one afternoon, and had reached the Village's zebra crossing. There was a car approaching, but with a lover's normal eagerness, I started to cross anyway. The car braked, harder than its driver had evidently wanted to, and hooted at me. I stopped where I was, right in line with the car's bonnet, and stared back at the driver. I admit I was perhaps an annoying sight. Long hair, purple jeans, and young—filthy, fucking young. The driver wound down his window and swore at me. I strolled round to him, smiling, and keen on confrontation. He was old—filthy, fucking old, with an old person's stupid red ears. You know those sorts of ears, all fleshy, with hairs growing on them inside and out? Thick, bristly ones inside; thin, furry ones outside.

"You'll be dead before I will," I informed him, and then dawdled off as irritatingly as I could manage.

So, now that I am older I realise that this is one of my human functions: to allow the young to believe that I envy them. Well, obviously I do in the brute matter of being dead first; but otherwise not. And when I see pairs of young lovers, vertically entwined on street corners, or horizontally entwined on a blanket in the park, the main feeling it arouses in me is a kind of protectiveness. No, not pity: protectiveness. Not that they would want my protection. And yet— and this is curious—the more bravado they show in their behaviour, the stronger my response. I want to protect them from what the world is probably going to do to them, and from what they will probably do to one another. But of course, this isn't possible. My care is not required, and their confidence insane.

• • •

It was a matter of some pride to me that I seemed to have landed on exactly the relationship of which my parents would most disapprove. I have no wish—certainly not at this late stage—to demonise them. They were products of their time and age and class and genes—just as I am. They were hardworking, truthful and wanted what they thought was the best for their only child. The faults I found in them were, in a different light, virtues. But at the time . . .

"Hi, Mum and Dad, I've something to tell you. I'm actually gay, which you probably guessed, and I'm going on holiday next week with Pedro. Yes, Mum, that Pedro, the one who does your hair in the Village. Well, he asked me where I was going for my holidays, and I just said, 'Any suggestions?' and we took it from there. So we're off to a Greek island together."

I imagine my parents being upset, and wondering what the neighbours would say, and going to ground for a while, and talking behind closed doors, and theorising difficulties ahead for me which would only be a projection of their own confused feelings. But then they would decide that times were changing, and find a little quiet heroism in their ability to accommodate this unanticipated situation, and my mother would wonder how socially appropriate it would be to let Pedro carry on cutting her hair, and then—

worst stage of all—she would award herself a badge of honour for her newfound tolerance, all the while giving thanks to the God in whom she did not believe that her father hadn't lived to see the day . . .

Yes, that would have been all right, eventually. As would another scenario then popular in the newspapers.

"Hi, Parents, this is Cindy, she's my girlfriend, well, actually a little bit more than that, as you can see, she's going to be a 'gymslip mum' in a few months' time. Don't worry, she was dead legal when I swooped at the school gates, but I guess the clock's ticking on this one, so you'd better meet her parents and book the registry office."

Yes, they could have coped with that too. Of course, their best-case scenario, as previously noted, was that down at the tennis club I would meet a nice Christine or Virginia whose emollient and optimistic nature would have been to their taste. And then there could have been a proper engagement followed by a proper wedding and a proper honeymoon, leading to proper grandchildren. But instead I had gone to the tennis club and come back with Mrs. Susan Macleod, a married woman of the parish with two daughters, both older than me. And—until such time as I shrugged off this foolish case of calf love—there would be no engagement or wedding, let alone patter of tiny feet. There would only be embarrassment and humiliation and shame, and prim looks from neighbours and sly allusions to cradle-snatching. So I had managed to present them with a case so far beyond the pale that it could not even be admitted, much less sensibly discussed. And by now, my mother's original idea of inviting the Macleods round for sherry had been definitively junked.

This thing with parents. All my friends at university—Eric, Barney, Ian and Sam—had it in varying amounts. And we were hardly a pack of stoned hippies in shaggy Afghan coats. We were normal—normalish—middle-class boys feeling the irritable rub of growing up. We all had our stories, most of them interchangeable, though Barney's were always the best. Not least because he gave his parents so much lip.

"So," Barney told us, as we reassembled for another term, and were exchanging dismal tales of Life at Home. "I'd been back about three weeks, and it's ten in the morning and I'm still in bed. Well, there's nothing to get up for in Pinner, is there? Then I hear the bedroom door open, and my mum and dad come in. They sit on the end of my bed, and Mum starts asking me if I know what time it is."

"Why can't they learn to knock?" asked Sam. "You might have been in mid-wank."

"So, naturally I said that it was probably

morning by my reckoning. And then they asked what I was planning to do that day, and I said I wasn't going to think about it till after breakfast. My dad gave this sort of dry cough—it's always a sign that he's starting to boil up. Then my mum suggests I might get a holiday job to earn a little pin money. So I admit that it hadn't exactly crossed my mind to apply for temporary employment in some menial trade."

"Nice one, Barney," we chorused.

"And then my mum asked if I was planning to idle away my whole life, and you know, I was beginning to get annoyed—I'm like my father in that, slow burn, except I don't give that little warning cough. Anyway, my dad suddenly loses it, stands up, rips open the curtains and shouts,

" 'We don't want you treating this place like a fucking hotel!' "

"Oh, *that* old one. We've all had that. So what did you say?"

"I said, 'If this *was* a fucking hotel, the fucking management wouldn't burst into my room at ten in the morning and sit on my fucking bed and bollock me.' "

"Barney, you ace!"

"Well, it was very provoking, I thought."

"Barney, you ace!"

So the Macleod household consisted of Susan, Mr. E.P., and two daughters, both away at university, known as Miss G. and Miss N.S. There was an old char who came twice a week, Mrs. Dyer; she had poor eyesight for cleaning but perfect vision for stealing vegetables and pints of milk. But who else came to the house? No friends were mentioned. Each weekend, Macleod played a round of golf; Susan had the tennis club. In all the times I joined them for supper, I never met anyone else.

I asked Susan who their friends were. She replied, in a casually dismissive tone I hadn't noted before, "Oh, the girls have friends—they bring them home from time to time."

This hardly seemed an adequate response. But a week or so later, Susan told me we were going to visit Joan.

"You drive," she said, handing me the keys to the Macleods' Austin. This felt like promotion, and I was fastidious with my gear-changing.

Joan lived about three miles away, and was the surviving sister of Gerald, who donkey's years previously had been sweet on Susan, but then had died suddenly from leukaemia, which was beastly luck. Joan had looked after their father until his death and had never married; she liked dogs and took an afternoon gin or two.

We parked in front of a squat, half-timbered house behind a beech hedge. Joan had a cigarette on when she answered the door, embraced Susan and looked at me inquisitively.

"This is Paul. He's driving me today. I really need my eyes testing, I think it's time for a new prescription. We met at the tennis club."

Joan nodded, and said, "I've shut the yappers up."

She was a large woman in a pastel-blue trouser suit; she had tight curls, brown lipstick, and was approximately powdered. She led us into the sitting room and collapsed into an armchair with a footstool in front of it. Joan was probably about five years older than Susan, but struck me as a generation ahead. On one arm of her chair was a face-down book of crosswords, on the other a brass ashtray held in place by weights concealed in a leather strap. The ashtray looked precariously full to me. No sooner had Joan sat down than she was up again.

"Join me in a little one?"

"Too early for me, darling."

"You're not exactly driving," Joan replied grumpily. Then, looking at me, "Drink, young sir?"

"No thank you."

"Well, suit yourselves. At least you'll have a gasper with me."

Susan, to my surprise, took a cigarette and lit up. It felt to me like a friendship whose hierarchy had been established long ago, with Joan as senior partner and Susan, if not subservient, at any rate the listening one. Joan's opening monologue told of her life since she'd last seen Susan, which seemed to me largely a catalogue of small annoyances triumphantly overcome, of dog-talk and bridge-talk, which resolved itself into the headline news that she had recently found a place ten miles away where you could get her favourite gin for some trifling sum less than it cost in the Village.

Bored out of my skull, half-disapproving of the cigarette Susan appeared to be enjoying, I found the following words coming out of my mouth:

"Have you factored in the petrol?"

It was as if my mother had spoken through me.

Joan looked at me with interest verging on approval. "Now, how would I do that?"

"Well, do you know how many mpg you get from your car?"

"Of course I do," Joan replied, as if it were outrageous and spendthrift not to know. "Twenty-eight on average around here, a bit over thirty on a longer trip."

"And how much do you pay for petrol?"

"Well, that obviously depends on where I buy it, doesn't it?"

"Aha!" I exclaimed, as if this made the matter even more interesting. "Another variable. Have you got a pocket calculator, by any chance?"

"I've got a screwdriver," said Joan, laughing.

"Pencil and paper, at least."

She fetched some and came to sit next to me on

the sofa, reeking of cigarettes. "I want to see this in action."

"So how many off-licences and how many petrol stations are we talking about?" I began. "I'll need the full details."

"Anyone would think you're from the Inland Fucking Revenue," said Joan with a laugh and a thump on my shoulder.

So I took down prices and locations and distances, identifying one case of spurious false economy, and came up with her two best options.

"Of course," I added brightly, "this one would be even more advantageous if you walked into the Village rather than drove."

Joan gave a mock shriek. "But walking's bad for me!" Then she took my table of calculations, went back to her chair, lit up another cigarette, and said to Susan, "I can see that he's a very useful young man to have around."

As we were driving away, Susan said, "Casey Paul, I didn't know you could be so wicked. You had her eating out of your hand by the end of it."

"Anything to help the rich save money," I replied, carefully shifting gear. "I'm your man."

"You *are* my man, strange as it may seem," she agreed, slipping her flattened hand beneath my left thigh as I drove.

"By the way, what's wrong with your eyes?"

"My eyes? Nothing, as far as I know."

"Then why did you go on about having them tested?"

"Oh, that? Well, I have to have a form of words to cover you."

Yes, I could see that. And so I became "the young man who drives me" and "my tennis partner," and later, "a friend of Martha's" and even—most implausibly—"a kind of protégé of Gordon's."

I don't remember when we first kissed. Isn't that odd? I can remember 6–2; 7–5; 2–6. I can remember that old driver's ears in foul detail. But I can't remember when or where we first kissed, or who made the first move, or whether it was both of us at the same time. And whether perhaps it was not so much a move as a drift. Was it in the car or in her house, was it morning, noon or night? And what was the weather like? Well, you certainly won't expect me to remember *that.*

All I can tell you is that it was—by the modern speed of things—a long time before we first kissed, and a long time after that before we first went to bed together. And that between the kissing and the bedding I drove her up to London to buy some contraception. For her, not me. We went to John Bell & Croyden in Wigmore Street; I parked round the corner while she went in. She returned with a brown, unbranded bag containing a Dutch cap and some contraceptive jelly.

"I wonder if there's a book of instructions," she says lightly. "I'm a bit out of practice with all this."

In my mood—a kind of sombre excitement—I'm momentarily unsure if she's referring to sex, or to putting in the cap.

"I'll be there to help," I say, thinking that this covers both interpretations.

"Paul," she says, "there are some things it's better for a man not to see. Or to think about."

"OK." This definitely means the second option.

"Where will you keep it?" I ask, imagining the consequences of its discovery.

"Oh, somewhere-somewhere," she replies. None of my business, then.

"Don't expect too much of me, Casey," she goes on rapidly. "Casey. That's K.C. King's Cross. You won't be a crosspatch, will you? You won't get all ratty and shirty with me, will you?"

I lean across and kiss her, in front of whatever interested pedestrians Wimpole Street contains.

I know already that she and her husband have separate beds, indeed separate rooms, and their marriage has been unconsummated—or rather, sex-free—for almost twenty years; but I haven't pressed her for reasons or particulars. On the one hand, I am deeply curious about almost everybody's sex life, past, present and future. On the other, I don't fancy the distraction of other images in my head when I am with her.

42

I am surprised that she needs contraception, that at forty-eight she is still having periods, and that what she refers to as The Dreaded has not yet arrived. But I am rather proud that it hasn't. This is nothing to do with the possibility that she might get pregnant—nothing could be further from my thoughts or desires; rather it seems a confirmation of her womanliness. I was going to say girlishness; and perhaps that's more what I mean. Yes, she is older; yes, she knows more about the world. But in terms of—what shall I call it? the age of her spirit, perhaps—we aren't that far apart.

"I didn't know you smoked," I say.

"Oh, just the one, occasionally. To keep Joan company. Or I go out into the garden. Do you disapprove terribly?"

"No, it just came as a surprise. I don't disapprove. I just think—"

"It's stupid. Yes it is. I just take one of his when I'm fed up. Have you noticed the way he smokes? He lights up and puffs away as if his life depends upon it, and then, when he's halfway through, he stubs it out in disgust. And that disgust lasts until he lights up the next one. About five minutes later."

Yes, I have noticed, but I let it go.

"Still, it's his drinking that's more annoying."

"But you don't?"

"I hate the stuff. Just a glass of sweet sherry at Christmas, so as not to be accused of being a spoilsport. But it changes people. And not for the better."

I agree. I have no interest in alcohol, or in people getting "merry," or "whistled," or "half seas over" and all the other words and phrases which make them feel better about themselves.

And Mr. E.P. was no exemplar of the virtues of drinking. While waiting for his dinner, he would sit at the table surrounded by what Susan called "his flagons and his gallons," pouring from them into his pint mug with an increasingly unsteady hand. In front of him was another mug, stuffed with spring onions, on which he would munch. Then, after a while, he would belch quietly, covering his mouth in a pseudo-genteel manner. As a consequence, I have loathed spring onions for most of my life. And never thought much of beer either.

"You know, I was thinking the other day that I haven't seen his eyes for years. Not really. Not for years and years. Isn't that strange? They're always hidden behind his glasses. And of course I'm never there when he takes them off at night. Not that I want to see them especially. I've seen enough of them. I expect it's the same for a lot of women."

This is how she tells me about herself, in

44

oblique observations which don't require a response. Sometimes, one leads on to another; sometimes, she lets drop a single statement, as if clueing me in to life.

"The thing you have to understand, Paul, is that we're a played-out generation."

I laugh. My parents' generation don't seem at all played out to me: they still have all the power and money and self-assurance. I wish they *were* played out. Instead, they seem a major obstacle to my growing up. What's that term they use in hospitals? Yes, bed-blockers. They were spiritual bed-blockers.

I ask Susan to explain.

"We went through the war," she says. "It took a lot out of us. We aren't much good for anything anymore. It's time your lot took charge. Look at our politicians."

"You aren't suggesting I go into politics?" I am incredulous. I despise politicians, who all strike me as self-important creeps and smoothies. Not that I've ever met a politician, of course.

"It's exactly because people like you don't go into politics that we're in the mess we are," Susan insists.

Again, I am baffled. I'm not even sure who "people like me" might be. For my school and university friends, it seemed like a badge of honour *not* to be interested in all the matters which politicians endlessly discussed. And then their grand anxieties—the Soviet threat, the End of Empire, tax rates, death duties, the housing crisis, trade union power—would be endlessly regurgitated at the family hearth.

My parents enjoyed television sitcoms, but were made uneasy by satire. You couldn't buy *Private Eye* in the Village, but I would bring it back from university and leave it provocatively around the house. I remember one issue whose cover had a floppy 33 rpm disk loosely attached to it. Peeling off the record revealed the photo of a man sitting on the lavatory, trousers and pants round his ankles, shirttails keeping him decent. On to the neck of this anonymous squatter was montaged the head of the Prime Minister, Sir Alec Douglas-Home, with a bubble coming out of his mouth saying, "Put that record back at once!" I found it supremely funny, and showed it to my mother; she judged it stupid and puerile. Then I showed it to Susan, who was overcome with laughter. So that was everything decided, in one go: me, my mother, Susan and politics.

She laughs at life, this is part of her essence. And no one else in her played-out generation does the same. She laughs at what I laugh at. She also laughs at hitting me on the head with a tennis ball; at the idea of having sherry with my parents; she laughs at her husband, just as she does when

46

crashing the gears of the Austin shooting brake. Naturally, I assume that she laughs at life because she has seen a great deal of it, and understands it.

"By the way," I say, "what's 'whatski'?"

"What do you mean, 'What's whatski'?"

"I mean, What's 'whatski'?"

"Oh, do you mean, 'Whatski's whatski'?"

"If you like."

"It's what Russian spies say to one another, silly," she replies.

The first time we were together—sexually, I mean—we each told the necessary lies, then drove across to the middle of Hampshire and found two rooms in a hotel.

As we stand looking down at an acreage of magenta candlewick bedspread, she says,

"Which side do you prefer? Forehand or back-hand?"

I have never slept in a double bed before. I have never slept a whole night with someone before. The bed looks enormous, the lighting bleak, and from the bathroom comes a smell of disinfectant.

"I love you," I tell her.

"That's a terrible thing to say to a girl," she replies and takes my arm. "We'd best have dinner first, before we love one another."

I already have an erection, and there is nothing generalised about this one. It is very, very specific.

She has a shyness to her. She never undresses in front of me; she is always in bed with her nightdress on by the time I come into the room. And the light would be out. I couldn't care less about any of this. I feel I can see in the dark, anyway.

Nor does she "teach me the arts of love," that phrase you read in books. We are both inexperienced, as I said. And she comes from a generation in which the assumption is made that on the wedding night the man "will know what to do"—a social excuse to legitimise any previous sexual experience, however squalid, the man might have had. I don't want to go into the specifics in her case, though she does occasionally drop hints.

One afternoon, we are in bed at their house, and I suggest I ought to be going before "Someone" comes home.

"Of course," she replies musingly. "You know, when he was at school, he always preferred the front half of the elephant, if you catch my meaning. And maybe after school. Who knows? Everyone's got a secret, haven't they?"

"What's yours?"

"Mine? Oh, he told me I was frigid. Not at the time. But later, after we'd stopped. When it was too late to do anything about anything."

"I don't think you're remotely frigid," I say,

with a mixture of outrage and possessiveness. "I think you're . . . very warm-blooded."

She pats my chest in reply. I know little about the female orgasm, and somehow assume that if you manage to keep going long enough, it will at some point be automatically triggered in the woman. Like breaking the sound barrier, perhaps. As I am unable to take the discussion further, I start to get dressed. Later, I think: she is warm, she is affectionate, she loves me, she encourages me into bed, we stay there a long time, *I* don't think she's frigid, what's the problem?

We talk about everything: the state of the world (not good), the state of her marriage (not good), the general character and moral standards of the Village (not good) and even Death (not good).

"Isn't it strange?" she muses. "My mother died of cancer when I was ten and I only ever think of her when I'm cutting my toenails."

"And yourself?"

"Whatski?"

"Yourself—dying."

"Oh." She goes silent for a bit. "No, I'm not afraid of dying. My only regret would be missing out on what happens afterwards."

I misunderstand her. "You mean, the afterlife?"

"Oh, I don't believe in *that*," she says firmly. "It would all cause far too much trouble. All those people who spent their lives getting away

49

from one another, and suddenly there they all are again, like some dreadful bridge party."

"I didn't know you played bridge."

"I don't. That's not the point, Paul. And then, all those people who did bad things to you. Seeing them again."

I leave a pause; she fills it. "I had an uncle. Uncle Humph. For Humphrey. I used to go and stay with him and Aunt Florence. After my mother died, so I would have been eleven, twelve. My aunt would put me to bed and tuck me in and kiss me and put out the light. And just as I would be getting off to sleep, there was a sudden weight on the side of the bed and it would be Uncle Humph, stinking of brandy and cigars and saying he wanted a goodnight kiss too. And then one time he said, 'Do you know what a "party kiss" is?' and before I could reply he rammed his tongue into my mouth and thrashed it around like a live fish. I wish I'd bitten it off. Every summer he did it, till I was about sixteen. Oh, it wasn't as bad as for some, I know, but maybe that's what made me frigid."

"You're *not,*" I insist. "And with a bit of luck the old bastard will be in a very hot place. If there's any justice."

"There isn't," she replies. "There isn't any justice, here or anywhere else. And the afterlife would just be an enormous bridge party with Uncle Humph bidding six no trumps and winning every hand and claiming a party kiss as his reward."

"I'm sure you're the expert," I say teasingly.

"But the thing *is,* Casey Paul, it would be dreadful, entirely dreadful, if in some way that man was still alive. And what you don't wish for your enemies, you can hardly expect for yourself."

I don't know when the habit developed—early on, I'm sure—but I used to hold her wrists. Maybe it began in a game of seeing if I could encompass them with my middle fingers and thumbs. But it rapidly became something I did. She extends her forearms towards me, fingers making gentle fists, and says, "Hold my wrists, Paul." I encompass them both, and press as hard as I can. What the exchange was about didn't need words. It was a gesture to calm her, to pass something from me to her. An infusion, a transfusion of strength. And of love.

My attitude to our love was peculiarly straightforward—though I suspect a peculiar straightforwardness is characteristic of all first love. I simply thought: Well, that's the certainty of love between us settled, now the rest of life has to fall into place around it. And I was entirely confident that it would. I remembered from some of my school reading that Passion was meant to Thrive on Obstacles; but now that I was experiencing what I had only previously read about, the notion of an Obstacle to it seemed neither necessary nor desirable. But I was very young, emotionally, and perhaps simply blind to the obstacles others would find in plain sight.

Or perhaps I didn't go by way of previous reading at all. Perhaps my actual thought was more like this: Here we are now, the two of us, and there is where we have to get to; nothing else matters. And though we did in the end get somewhere near to where I dreamed, I had no idea of the cost.

I said I couldn't remember the weather. And there's other stuff as well, like what clothes I wore and what food I ate. Clothes were unimportant necessities back then, and food was just fuel. Nor do I remember things I'd expect to, like the colour of the Macleods' shooting brake. I think it was two-tone. But was it grey and green, or perhaps blue and cream? And though I spent many key hours on its leather seats, I couldn't tell you their colour. Was the fascia panel made of walnut? Who cares? My memory certainly doesn't, and it's memory which is my guide here.

On top of this, there are things I can't be bothered to tell you. Like what I studied at university, what my room there was like, and how Eric differed from Barney, and Ian from Sam, and which one of them had red hair. Except that

Eric was my closest friend, and continued so for many years. He was the gentlest of us, the most thoughtful, the one who put most trust in others. And—perhaps because of these very qualities—he was the one who had most trouble with girls and, later, women. Was there something about his softness, and his inclination to forgive, which almost provoked bad behaviour in others? I wish I knew the answer to that, not least because of the time I let him down badly. I abandoned him when he needed my help; I betrayed him, if you will. But I'll tell you about this later.

And another thing. When I gave you my estate agent's sketch of the Village, some of it might not have been strictly accurate. For instance, the Belisha beacons at the zebra crossing. I might have invented them, because nowadays you rarely see a zebra crossing without a dutiful pair of flashing beacons. But back then, in Surrey, on a road with little traffic . . . I rather doubt it. I suppose I could do some real-life research—look for old postcards in the central library, or hunt out the very few photos I have from that time, and retrofit my story accordingly. But I'm remembering the past, not reconstructing it. So there won't be much set-dressing. You might prefer more. You might be used to more. But there's nothing I can do about that. I'm not trying to spin you a story; I'm trying to tell you the truth.

• • •

Susan's tennis game comes back to me. Mine—as I may have said—was largely a self-taught business, relying on wristiness, ill-prepared body position and a deliberate, last-minute change of shot which sometimes bamboozled me as much as my opponent. When playing with her, this structural laziness often compromised my intense desire for victory. Her game had schooling behind it: she got into the correct position, hit fully through her groundstrokes, came to the net only when circumstances were propitious, ran her socks off and yet laughed equally at winning and losing. This had been my first impression of her, and from her tennis I naturally extrapolated her character. I assumed that in life too she would be calm, well ordered and reliable, hitting fully through the ball—the best possible backcourt support for her anxious and impulsive partner at the net.

We entered the mixed doubles in the club's summer tournament. There were about three people watching our first-round match against a couple of old hackers in their mid-fifties; to my surprise, one of the spectators was Joan. Even when we changed ends and she was out of my eyeline, I could hear her smoker's cough.

The old hackers hacked us to death, playing like a married couple who could instinctively read one another's next move, and never needed to speak, let alone shout. Susan played solidly, as ever, whereas my game was stupidly erratic. I went for overambitious interceptions, took balls I should have left, and then fell into a lethargic sulk as the hackers closed out set and match 6–4.

Afterwards, we sat with Joan, two teas and a gin between the three of us.

"Sorry I let you down," I said.

"That's all right, Paul, I really don't mind."

Her even temper made me more irritated with myself. "No, but I do. I was trying all sorts of stupid stuff. I wasn't any help. And I couldn't get my first serve in."

"You let your left shoulder drop," said Joan out of the blue.

"But I serve right-handed," I replied rather petulantly.

"That's why the left shoulder has to be kept high. Holds you in balance."

"I didn't know you played."

"Played? Ha! I used to win the fucking thing. Until my knees went. You need a few lessons, young Master Paul, that's all. But you've got good hands."

"Look—he's blushing!" Susan observed unnecessarily. "I've never seen him do that before."

Later, in the car, I say, "So what's Joan's story? Was she really a good player?"

"Oh yes. She and Gerald won pretty much

55

everything, up to county level. She was a strong singles player, as you can probably imagine, until her knees let her down. But she was even better at doubles. Having someone to support and be supported by."

"I like Joan," I say. "I like the way she swears."

"Yes, that's what people see and hear, and like or don't like. Her gin, her cigarettes, her bridge game, her dogs. Her swearing. Don't underestimate Joan."

"I wasn't," I protest. "Anyway, she said I had good hands."

"Don't always be joking, Paul."

"Well, I *am* only nineteen, as my parents keep reminding me."

Susan goes quiet for a bit, then, seeing a lay-by, turns into it and stops the car. She looks ahead through the windscreen.

"When Gerald died, I wasn't the only one who was hard hit. Joan was devastated. They'd lost their mother when they were little, and their father had to work every day in that insurance company, so they were thrown into depending on one another. And when Gerald died . . . she went off the rails a bit. Started sleeping with people."

"There's nothing wrong with that."

"There is and there isn't, Casey Paul. Depends on who you are and who they are. And who's robust enough to survive. Usually, that's the man."

"Joan seems pretty robust to me."

"That's an act. We all have an act. You'll have an act one day, oh yes you will. So Joan was a bad picker. And at first it didn't seem to matter, as long as she didn't get pregnant or anything like that. And she didn't. Then she fell like a ton of bricks for . . . his name doesn't matter. Married of course, rich of course, other girlfriends of course. Set her up at a flat in Kensington."

"Good Lord. Joan was . . . a kept woman? A . . . mistress?" These were words, and sexual functions, I'd only come across in books.

"Whatever you want to call it. The words don't fit. They rarely do. What do you call you? What do you call me?" I don't reply. "And Joan was completely gone on the old bastard. Waiting for his visits, believing his promises, going off on the occasional weekend abroad. He strung her along like that for three years. Then at last, as he'd always promised, he divorced his wife. And Joan thought her ship had come home. She'd proved us all wrong, what's more. 'My ship's coming home,' she kept repeating."

"But it hadn't?"

"He married another woman instead. Joan read the announcement in the papers. Piled up all the clothes he'd bought her in the sitting room of the flat, poured lighter fuel over them, lit a match, walked out, slammed the door, put the keys through the letterbox, went back to her father.

Turned up on his doorstep. Smelt a bit singed, I expect. Her father didn't say anything or ask any questions, just hugged her. It took her months even to tell him. The only luck—if there was luck—was that she didn't set the whole block of flats on fire. Just burnt a hole in an expensive carpet. She could have ended up in prison for manslaughter.

"After that she took care of her father devotedly. Became interested in dogs. Had a go at breeding them. Learned how to pass the time. That's one of the things about life. We're all just looking for a place of safety. And if you don't find one, then you have to learn how to pass the time."

I don't think this will ever be my problem. Life is just too full and always will be.

"Poor old Joan," I say. "I'd never have guessed."

"She cheats at crosswords."

This seems a non sequitur to me.

"What?"

"She cheats at crosswords. She does them out of books. She once told me that if she gets stuck, she fills in any old word, as long as it's the right number of letters."

"But that defeats the whole purpose . . . and anyway, all the answers are in the back of those books." I am at a loss, so just repeat, "Poor old Joan."

"Yes and no. Yes and no. But don't ever forget,

young Master Paul. Everyone has their love story. Everyone. It may have been a fiasco, it may have fizzled out, it may never even have got going, it may have been all in the mind, that doesn't make it any less real. Sometimes, it makes it more real. Sometimes, you see a couple, and they seem bored witless with one another, and you can't imagine them having anything in common, or why they're still living together. But it's not just habit or complacency or convention or anything like that. It's because once, they had their love story. Everyone does. It's the only story."

I don't answer. I feel rebuked. Not rebuked by Susan. Rebuked by life.

That evening, I looked at my parents and paid attention to everything they said to one another. I tried to imagine that they too had had their love story. Once upon a time. But I couldn't get anywhere with that. Then I tried imagining that each had had their love story, but separately, either before marriage or perhaps—even more thrillingly—during it. But I couldn't make that work either, so I gave up. I found myself wondering instead if, like Joan, I would one day have an act of my own, an act designed to deflect curiosity. Who could tell?

Then I went back and tried to imagine how it might have been for my parents in those years before I had existed. I picture them starting off together, side by side, hand in hand, happy, confident, strolling down some gentle, soft, grassy furrow. All is verdant and the view extensive; there seems to be no hurry. Then, as life proceeds, in its normal, daily, unthreatening way, the furrow very slowly deepens, and the green becomes flecked with brown. A little further on—a decade or two—and the earth is heaped higher on either side, and they are unable to see over the top. And now there is no escape, no turning back. There is only the sky above, and ever-higher walls of brown earth, threatening to entomb them.

Whatever happened, I wasn't going to be a furrow-dweller. Or a breeder of dogs.

"What you have to understand is this," she says. "There were three of us. The boys got the education—that's how it was. Philip's took him all the way, but the money for Alec ran out when he was fifteen. Alec was the one I was closest to. Everyone adored Alec, he was just the best. Naturally, he joined up as soon as he could, that's what the best ones did. The Air Force. He ended up flying Sunderlands. They're flying boats. They used to go out on long patrols over the Atlantic, looking for U-boats. Thirteen hours at a time. They gave them pills to help them keep going. No, that's nothing to do with it.

"So, you see, on his last leave he took me to supper. Nowhere posh, just Corner House. And he took my hands in his and said, 'Sue darling, they're complicated beasts, those Sunderlands, and I often don't think I'm up to it. They're too bloody complicated, and sometimes, when you're out there over the water, and it all looks the same, hour after hour, you've no idea where you are, and sometimes even the navigator doesn't either. I always say a prayer at takeoff and landing. I don't believe, but I say a prayer nevertheless. And every time I'm just as bloody scared as the time before. Right, I've got that off my chest. Corners up from now on. Corners up in the Corner House.'

"That was the last time I saw him. He was posted missing three weeks later. They never found a trace of his plane. And I always think of him out there, over the water, being scared."

I put my arm around her. She shakes it loose, frowningly.

"No, that's not all. There always seemed to be these men around. It was wartime and you'd think they'd all be off fighting, but there was a jolly lot of them around at home, I can tell you. The lesser men. So there was Gerald, who couldn't pass the medical, even though he tried twice, and then Gordon, who was in a reserved occupation, as he liked to say. Gerald was sweet-tempered and nice-looking, and Gordon was a bit of a crosspatch, but anyway I just preferred dancing with Gerald. Then we got engaged, because,

61

well, it was wartime and people did things like that then. I don't think I was in love with Gerald, but he was a kind man, that's for sure. And then he went and died of leukaemia. I told you that. It was beastly luck. So I thought I might as well marry Gordon. I thought it might make him less of a crosspatch. And *that* part of things didn't work out, as you may have observed."

"But—"

"*So,* you see, we're a played-out generation. All the best ones went. We were left with the lesser ones. It's always like that in war. That's why it's up to your generation now."

But I don't feel part of a generation, for a start; and, moved as I am by her story, her history, her prehistory, I still don't want to go into politics.

We were driving somewhere in my car, a Morris Minor convertible in a shade of mud-green. Susan said it looked like a very low-level German staff car from the war. We were at the foot of a long hill, with no traffic in sight. I was never a reckless driver, but I pushed hard down on the accelerator pedal to get a good run at the gradient. And after about fifty yards I realised something was seriously wrong. The car was accelerating at full throttle, even though I'd now taken my foot off the pedal. Instinctively, I rammed it on the brake. That didn't help much. I was doing two things at the same time: panicking, and thinking clearly. Don't ever believe those two states are incompatible. The engine was roaring, the brakes were screaming, the car was beginning to slew across the road, we were going between forty and fifty. It never occurred to me to ask Susan what to do. I thought, this is my problem, I've got to fix it. And then it came to me: take the car out of gear. So I put in the clutch, and moved the gear stick to neutral. The car's hysteria decreased and we coasted to a halt on the verge.

"Well done, Casey Paul," she says. Giving me both names was usually a sign of approval.

"I should have thought of that earlier. Actually, I should have just switched off the bloody ignition. That would have done it. But it didn't cross my mind."

"I think there's a garage over the hill," she says, getting out, as if such an event were entirely routine.

"Were you scared?"

"No. I knew you'd sort it out, whatever it was. I always feel safe with you."

I remember her saying that, and me feeling proud. But I also remember the feel of the car as it raced out of control, as it resisted the brakes, as it bucked and slewed across the road.

I must tell you about her teeth. Well, two of them, anyway. The middle front ones at the top. She called them her "rabbit teeth" because they were perhaps a millimetre longer than the strict national average; but that, to me, made them the more special. I used to tap them lightly with my middle finger, checking that they were there, and secure, just as she was. It was a little ritual, as if I was taking an inventory of her.

Everyone in the Village, every grown-up—or rather, every middle-aged person—seemed to do crosswords: my parents, their friends, Joan, Gordon Macleod. Everyone apart from Susan. They did either *The Times* or *The Telegraph*; though Joan had those books of hers to fall back on while waiting for the next newspaper. I regarded this traditional British activity with some snootiness. I was keen in those days to find hidden motives—preferably involving hypocrisy—behind the obvious ones. Clearly, this supposedly harmless pastime was about more than solving cryptic clues and filling in the answers. My analysis identified the following elements: 1) the desire to reduce the chaos of the universe to a small, comprehensible grid of black-and-white squares; 2) the underlying belief that everything in life could, in the end, be solved; 3) the confirmation that existence was essentially a ludic activity; and 4) the hope that this activity would keep at bay the existential pain of our brief sublunary transit from birth to death. That seemed to cover it!

One evening, Gordon Macleod looked up from behind a cigarette smokescreen and asked,

"Town in Somerset, seven letters, ends in N."

I thought about this for a while. "Swindon?"

He made a tolerant tut-tut. "Swindon's in Wiltshire."

"Is it really? That's a surprise. Have you ever been there?"

"Whether I have or not is hardly relevant to the business in hand," he replied. "Look at it on the page. That might help."

I went and sat next to him. Seeing a lineup of six blank spaces followed by an N didn't help me any the more.

"Taunton," he announced, putting in the answer. I noticed the eccentric way he did his capital letters, lifting the pen from the page to make each stroke. Whereas anyone else would produce an N from two applications of pen to paper, he made three.

"Continue mocking Somerset town. That was the clue."

I thought about this, not very hard, admittedly.

"Taunt on—continue mocking. Taunt on—TAUNTON. Get it, young fellermelad?"

"Oh, *I see,*" I said nodding. "That's clever."

I didn't mean it, of course. I was also thinking that Macleod must certainly have got the answer before he asked me. So then I added an extra clause to my analysis of the crossword—or, as

Macleod preferred to call it, The Puzzle: 3b) false confirmation that you are more intelligent than some give you credit for.

"Does Mrs. Macleod do the crossword?" I asked, already knowing the answer. Two could play at this game, I thought.

"The Puzzle," he replied with some archness, "is not really a female domain."

"My mum does the crossword with my dad. Joan does the crossword."

He lowered his chin and looked at me over his spectacles.

"Then let us posit, perhaps, that The Puzzle is not the domain of the womanly woman. What do you say to that?"

"I'd say I don't have enough experience of life to come to a conclusion on that one." Though inwardly I was reflecting on the phrase "womanly woman." Was it uxorious praise, or some kind of disguised insult?

"So that gives us an O in the middle of twelve down," he went on. Suddenly there was an "us" involved.

I gazed at the clue. Something about an arbiter in work and a leaf.

"TREFOIL," Macleod muttered, writing it in, three strokes of his pen on the R, where others would construct it from two. "You see, it's REF—arbiter—in the middle of TOIL—work."

"That's clever too," I falsely enthused.

"Standard. Had it before a few times," he added with a touch of complacency.

2b) the further belief that once you have solved something in life, you will be able to solve it again, and the solution will be exactly the same the second time around, thus offering assurance that you have reached a pitch of maturity and wisdom.

Macleod decided, without my asking, to teach me the ins and outs of The Puzzle. Anagrams, and how to spot them; words hidden inside other combinations of words; setters' shorthand and their favourite tricks; common abbreviations, letters and words drawn from chess annotation, military ranks, and so on; how a word may be written upwards in the solution to a down clue, or backwards in an across clue. " 'Running west,' you see, that's the giveaway."

Correction to 4). To begin: "the hope that this arse-bendingly boring activity would keep . . ."

Later, I tried making an anagram out of WOMANLY WOMAN. I didn't get anywhere, of course. WANLY MOWN LOOM and other bits of nonsense were all I turned up.

Further addition: 1a) a successful means of taking your mind off the question of love, which is all that counts in the world.

Nonetheless, I continued to keep Macleod company while he puffed away at his Players and filled his grids with strangely mechanical pen strokes. He seemed to enjoy explaining clues to me, and took my occasional half-meant whistles and grunts as applause.

"We'll make a Puzzle-solver of him yet," he remarked to Susan over supper one evening.

Sometimes, we did things together, he and I. Nothing major, or for a long time, anyway. He asked me for my help with some rope-and-pin instrument in the garden, designed to ensure that the cabbages he was planting out were in regimental lines. A couple of times, we listened to a test match on the radio. Once, he took me with him to fill up the car with what he referred to as "petroleum." I asked which garage he was intending to patronise. The nearest, he told me, unsurprisingly. I told him that I had done an analysis of price versus distance in the matter of Joan's gin, and what my findings had been.

"How incredibly boring," he commented, and then smiled at me.

I realised that I had seen his eyes on more than one occasion recently. Whereas Susan hadn't seen them in years. Maybe she was exaggerating. Or maybe she hadn't been looking too hard in the first place.

NOW ONLY MMWAA . . . no, that wasn't any good either.

Here is something I often thought at this time: I've been educated at school and university, and yet, in real terms, I know nothing. Susan barely went to school, but she knows so much more. I've got the book-learning, she's got the life-learning.

Not that I always agreed with her. When she was talking about Joan, she'd said: "We're all just looking for a place of safety." I pondered these words for a while afterwards. The conclusion I came to was this: maybe so, but I'm young, I'm "only nineteen," and I'm more interested in looking for a place of danger.

Like Susan, I had euphemistic phrases to describe our relationship. We just seem to have this rapport across the generations. She's my tennis partner. We both like music and go up to London for concerts. Also, art exhibitions. Oh, I don't know, we just get on somehow. I have no idea who believed what, and who knew what, and how much my pride made it all flauntingly obvious. Nowadays, at the other end of life, I have a rule of thumb about whether or not two people are having an affair: if you think they might be, then they definitely are. But this was decades ago, and perhaps, back then, the couples you thought might be, mainly weren't.

And then there were the daughters. I wasn't much at ease with girls at that time of my life, neither the ones I met at university, nor the Carolines at the tennis club. I didn't understand that they were mostly just as nervous as I was about . . . the whole caboodle. And while boys were good at coming up with their own, homemade bullshit, girls, in their understanding of the world, often seemed to fall back on The Wisdom of Their Mothers. You could sniff the inauthenticity when a girl—knowing no more than you did about anything—said something like: "Everyone's got twenty-twenty vision with hindsight." A line which could have issued word for word from the mouth of my mother. Another piece of appropriated maternal wisdom I remember from this time was this: "If you lower your expectations, you can't be disappointed." This struck me as a dismal approach to life, whether for a forty-five-year-old mother or a twenty-year-old daughter.

But anyway: Martha and Clara. Miss G. and Miss N.S. Miss Grumpy and Miss Not So (Grumpy). Martha was like her mother physically, tall and pretty, but with something of her father's querulous temperament. Clara was plump and round, but entirely more equable. Miss Grumpy disapproved of me; Miss Not So was friendly, even interested. Miss Grumpy said things like, "Haven't you got a home of your own to go to?" Miss Not So would ask what I was reading and once, even, showed me some poetry she'd written. But I wasn't much of a judge of poetry, then or now, so my response probably disappointed her. This was my preliminary assessment, for what it was worth.

If I was uneasy with girls generally, I was the more so with ones who were a bit older than me, let alone ones whose mother I was in love with. This awkwardness of mine seemed to emphasise the insouciance with which they moved about their own house, appeared, disappeared, spoke or failed to speak. My reaction to this was possibly a bit crude, but I decided to be no more interested in them than they were in me. This seemed to amount to less than a passing 5 percent. Which was fine by me, because more than 95 percent of my interest was in Susan.

Since Martha disapproved of me the more, it was to her, in a spirit of either challenge or perversity, that I said:

"I think I should explain. Susan's a kind of mother-substitute for me."

No, it wasn't very good, in any way. It probably sounded false, a slimy attempt at ingratiation. Martha took her time about replying, and her tone was acerbic.

"I don't need one, I've already got a mother."

Did I mean any part of my lie? I can't believe that I did. Strange as it may seem I never reflected on our age difference. Age felt as irrelevant as money. Susan never seemed a member of my parents' generation—"played-out" or not. She never pulled any sort of rank on me, never said,

"Ah, when you're a bit older, you'll understand" and stuff like that. It was only my parents who harped on about my immaturity.

Aha, you might say, but surely the fact that you told her own daughter that for you she was a mother-substitute is a complete giveaway? You may claim it was insincere, but don't we all make jokes to allay our inner fears? She was almost exactly the same age as your mother, and you went to bed with her. So?

So. I see where you're going—bus number 27 to a crossroads near Delphi. Look, I did not want, at any point, on any level, to kill my own father and sleep with my own mother. It's true that I wanted to sleep with Susan—and did so many times—and for a number of years thought of killing Gordon Macleod, but that is another part of the story. Not to put too fine a point on it, I think the Oedipus myth is precisely what it started off as: melodrama rather than psychology. In all my years of life I've never met anyone to whom it might apply.

You think I'm being naive? You wish to point out that human motivation is deviously buried, and hides its mysterious workings from those who blindly submit to it? Perhaps so. But even—especially—Oedipus didn't *want* to kill his father and sleep with his mother, did he? Oh yes he did! Oh no he didn't! Yes, let's just leave it as a pantomime exchange.

Not that prehistory doesn't matter. Indeed, I think prehistory is central to all relationships.

But I'd much rather tell you about her ears. I missed my first sight of them at the tennis club, when she had her hair pulled back by that green ribbon which matched the piping and buttons of her dress. And normally, she wore her hair down, curling over her ears and descending to mid-neck. So it wasn't until we were in bed and I was rummaging and rootling around her body, into every nook and cranny, every overexamined and underexamined part of her, that, crouched above, I swept back her hair and discovered her ears.

I'd never thought much about ears before, except as comic excrescences. Good ears were ears you didn't notice; bad ears stuck out like bat wings, or were cauliflowered from a boxer's punch, or—like those of that furious driver at the zebra crossing—were coarse and red and hairy. But her ears, ah, her ears . . . from the discreet, almost absent lobe they set off northwards at a gentle angle, but then at the midpoint turned back at the same angle to return to her skull. It was as if they had been designed according to aesthetic principle rather than the rules of auditory practicality.

When I point this out to her, she says, "It's probably so all that *rubbish* scoots past them and doesn't go inside."

But there was more. As I explored them with the tips of my fingers, I discovered the delicacy of their outer rim: thin, warm, gentle, almost translucent. Do you know the word for that outermost whorl of the ear? It's called the helix. Plural: helices. Her ears were part of her absolute distinctiveness, expressions of her DNA. The double helix of her double helices.

Later, turning my mind to what she might have meant by the "rubbish" that scooted past her astonishing ears, I thought: well, being accused of frigidity, that's a major piece of rubbish. Except that this word had gone straight into her ears and thence her brain and was lodged there, permanently.

As I said, money had no more relevance to our relationship than age. So it didn't matter that she paid for things. I had none of that foolish masculine pride in such circumstances. Perhaps I even felt my lack of money made my love for Susan the more virtuous.

After a few months—maybe longer—she announces that I need a running-away fund.

"What for?"

"For running away. Everyone should have a running-away fund." Just as every young man should have a reputation. Where had this latest idea come from? A Nancy Mitford novel?

"But I don't want to run away. Who from? My

parents? I've more or less left them anyway. Mentally. You? Why should I want to run away from you? I want you to be in my life forever."

"That's very sweet of you, Paul. But it's not a specific fund, you see. It's a sort of general fund. Because at some point everyone wants to run away from their life. It's about the only thing human beings have in common."

This is all way above my head. The only running away I might contemplate is running away with her rather than from her.

A few days later, she gives me a cheque for £500. My car had cost me £25; I lived for a term at university on under £100. The sum seemed both very large and also meaningless. I didn't even think it "generous." I had no principles about money, either for or against. And it was entirely irrelevant to our relationship—that much I knew. So when I got back to Sussex, I went into town, opened a deposit account at the first bank I came to, handed over the cheque and forgot about it.

There's something I probably should have clarified earlier. I may be making my relationship with Susan sound like a sweet summer interlude. That's what the stereotype insists, after all. There is a sexual and emotional initiation, a lush passage of treats and pleasures and spoilings, then the woman, with a pang but also a sense of honour, releases the young man back into the wider world and younger bodies of his own generation. But I've already told you that it wasn't like this.

We were together—and I mean together—for ten or a dozen years, depending on where you start and stop counting. And those years happened to coincide with what the newspapers liked to call the Sexual Revolution: a time of omni-fucking—or so we were led to believe—of instant pleasures, and loose, guilt-free liaisons, when deep lust and emotional lightness became the order of the day. So you could say that my relationship with Susan proved as offensive to the new norms as to the old ones.

I remember her, one afternoon, wearing a print dress with flowers on it, going over to a chintz sofa and plumping herself down on it.

"Look, Casey Paul! I'm disappearing! I'm doing my disappearing act! There's nobody here!"

I look. It is half-true. Her stockinged legs show clearly, as do her head and neck, but all the middle parts are suddenly camouflaged.

"Wouldn't you like that, Casey Paul? If we could just disappear and nobody could see us?"

I don't know how serious, or how merely skittish, she is being. So I don't know how to react. Looking back, I think I was a very literal young man.

• • •

I told Eric that I had met this family and fallen in love. I described the Macleods, their house and their way of life, relishing my characterizations. It was the first grown-up thing that had happened to me, I told him.

"So which of the daughters have you fallen in love with?" Eric asked.

"No, not one of the daughters, the mother."

"Ah, the mother," he said. "We like that," he added, giving me marks for originality.

One day, I notice a dark bruise on her upper arm, just below where the sleeve of her dress ends. It is the size of a large thumbprint.

"What's that?" I ask.

"Oh," she says carelessly, "I must have knocked it against something. I bruise easily."

Of course she does, I think. Because she's sensitive, like me. Of course the world can hurt us. That's why we must look after one another.

"You don't bruise when I hold your wrists."

"I don't think the wrists bruise, do they?"

"Not if I'm holding you."

The fact that she was "old enough to be my mother" did not go down well with my mother. Nor my father; nor her husband; nor her daughters; nor the Archbishop of Canterbury— not that he was a family friend. I cared no more about approval than I did about money. Though disapproval, whether active or theoretical, ignorant or informed, did nothing but inflame, corroborate and justify my love.

I had no new definition of love. I didn't really examine what it was, and what it might entail. I merely submitted to first love in all its aspects, from butterfly kisses to absolutism. Nothing else mattered. Of course there was "the rest of my life," both present (my degree course) and future (job, salary, social position, retirement, pension, death). You could say that I put this part of my life on hold. Except that's not right: she *was* my life, and the rest wasn't. Everything else could and must be sacrificed, with or without thought, as and when necessary. Though "sacrifice" implies loss. I never felt a sense of loss. Church and state, they say, church and state. No difficulty there. Church first, church always—though not in a sense the Archbishop of Canterbury would have understood it.

I wasn't so much constructing my own idea of love as first doing the necessary rubble clearance. Most of what I'd read, or been taught, about love, didn't seem to apply, from playground rumour to high-minded literary speculation. "Man's love is of man's life a thing apart/'Tis woman's whole existence." How wrong—how gender-biased, as we might now say—was that? And then, at the other end of the spectrum, came the earthy sex-wisdom exchanged between profoundly ignorant if yearningly lustful schoolboys. "You don't look at the mantelpiece while poking the fire." Where had that come from? Some bestial dystopia full of nocturnal, myopic grunting?

But I wanted her face there all the time: her eyes, her mouth, her precious ears with their elegant helices, her smile, her whispered words. So: I would be flat on my back, she would be lying on top of me, her feet slipped between mine, and she would place the tip of her nose against the tip of mine, and say,

"Now we see eye to eye."

Put it another way. I was nineteen, and I knew that love was incorruptible, proof against both time and tarnish.

I have a sudden attack of—what?—fear, propriety, unselfishness? I say to her, thinking she will know more,

"You see, I haven't been in love before, so I don't understand about love. What I'm worried about is that, if you love me, it will leave you less for the other people you love."

I don't name them. I meant her daughters; and perhaps even her husband.

"It's not like that," she answers at once, as if it is something she too has thought about, and has solved. "Love's elastic. It's not a question of watering down. It adds on. It doesn't take away. So there's no need to worry about that."

So I didn't.

"There's something I need to explain," she begins. "E.P.'s father was a very nice man. He was a doctor. He collected furniture. Some of these things were his." She points vaguely at a heavy oak coffer and a grandfather clock I have never yet heard strike the hour. "He actually hoped E.P. would become a painter, so he gave him the middle name of Rubens. Which was a bit unfortunate because some of the boys at school assumed he must be Jewish. Anyway, he did the usual schoolboy sketches, which everyone said were promising. But he never became more than promising, so was a disappointment to his father in that department. Jack—the father—was always very kind to me. He used to twinkle at me."

"I can't say I blame him for that." I wonder what might be coming next. Surely not some intergenerational imbroglio?

"We'd only been married a couple of years when Jack got cancer. I'd always thought he would be someone I could go to if I got in any trouble, and now he was going to be taken from me. I used to go and sit with him, but I would get so upset that it usually ended up with him consoling me rather than the other way round. I asked him once what he thought about it all, and he said, 'Of course I'd prefer it otherwise, but I can't complain that I haven't had a fair crack of the whip.' He liked me being with him, maybe because I was young and didn't know very much, and so I stayed there till the end.

"That day—the last day—the doctor—the one looking after him, who was a good friend as well—came in and said quietly, 'It's time to put you under, Jack.' 'You're right,' came the reply. He'd been in terrible pain for too long, you see. Then Jack turned to me and said, 'I'm sorry our acquaintance has been so brief, my dear. It's been wonderful knowing you. I'm aware that Gordon can be a difficult row to hoe, but I'll die happy knowing that I leave him in your safe and capable hands.' And then I kissed him and left the room."

"You mean, the doctor killed him?"

"He gave him enough morphine to put him to sleep, yes."

"But he didn't wake up?"

"No. Doctors used to do that in the old days, especially among themselves. Or with a patient they'd known a long time, where there was trust. Easing the suffering is a good idea. It's a terrible disease."

"Even so. I'm not sure I'd want to be killed."

"Well, wait and see, Paul. But that's not the point of the story."

"Sorry."

"The point of the story is 'safe and capable.' "

I think about this for a while. "Yes, I see." But I'm not sure that I did.

"Where do you usually go for your holidays?" I ask.

"Paul, that's such a hairdresser's question."

In reply, I lean over and tuck her hair behind her ears, stroking the helices gently.

"Oh dear," she goes on. "All these conventional expectations people have of one. No, not you, Casey Paul. I mean, why does everyone have to be the same? We did have a few holidays once, when the girls were young. About as successful as the Dieppe Raid, I'd say. E.P. was not at his best on holidays. I don't see what they're for, really."

I wonder if I shouldn't press any further. Perhaps something catastrophic had happened on one of their holidays.

"So what do you say when hairdressers ask you that question?"

"I say, 'We're still going to the usual place.' And that makes them think we've talked about it before and they've forgotten, so they usually let me off after that."

"Maybe you and I should have a holiday."

"You might have to teach me what they're for."

"What they're *for*," I say firmly, "is for being with someone you love a few hundred miles away from this sodding Village where we both live. Being with them all the time. Going to bed with them and waking up with them."

"Well, put like that, Casey . . ."

So you see, there were some things I knew and she didn't.

We are sitting in the cafeteria of the Festival Hall before a concert. Susan has noticed early on that when my blood sugar drops I become, in her words, "a bit of a grumpus," and she is now feeding me up to prevent this. I am probably having a something-and-chips; she will content herself with a cup of coffee and a few biscuits. I love these escapes we make up to London, just for a few hours, being together, away from the Village, from my parents and her husband and all that stuff, in the noise and crush of the city, waiting for the silence and then the sudden floatingness of music.

I am about to say all this when a woman comes and sits at our table without a pretence of asking if we mind. A woman of middle age, by herself; that is all she was, though in memory I might have translated her into some version of my mother—at any rate, a woman who could be counted upon to disapprove of my relationship with Susan. And so, after a couple of minutes, knowing exactly what I am doing, I look across and say to Susan, in a clear, exact voice,

"Will you marry me?"

She blushes, covers her ears and bites her lower lip. With a bang and a push and a stomp, the invader picks up her cup and makes for another table.

"Oh, Casey Paul," says Susan, "you are mighty wicked."

I was having supper at the Macleods'. Clara was there too, back from university. Macleod was at the head of the table with his flagon of whatever, a mugful of spring onions in front of him like a jar of tulips.

"You might be aware," he said to Clara, "that this young man appears to have joined our household. So be it."

I couldn't tell from his tone whether he was being pedantically welcoming or slyly indicating his disdain. I looked across at Clara, but got no help with interpretation.

"Well, we shall see, shan't we?" he continued, appearing to contradict his first pronouncement. He took in a mouthful of spring onion and shortly afterwards burped gently.

"One of the things the young man is kindly, if belatedly, addressing is the question of your mother's musical education. Or, should I say, lack thereof."

Then, turning to me: "Clara was named after Clara Schumann, which was perhaps a little ambitious on our part. She has never, alas, displayed much aptitude for the pianoforte, has she?"

I couldn't tell if the question was addressed to mother or daughter. As for me, I had never heard of Clara Schumann, so felt at even more of a disadvantage.

"Maybe, if your mother had begun her musical education earlier, she might have been able to pass on to you some of her now late-flowering enthusiasm."

I had never before been in a household in which the male presence was so overbearing and yet so ambiguous. Perhaps this happens when there is only one man around: his understanding of the male role can expand unchallenged. Or perhaps this was just what Gordon Macleod was like.

Still, my inability to grasp tone was a lesser matter that evening. The greater problem was that, at nineteen, I was unskilled at knowing how to behave socially at the table of a man whose wife I was in love with.

Dinner and conversation proceeded. Susan seemed half-absent; Clara was quiet. I asked a few polite questions and answered some rather more direct ones in return. As I had told the tennis club's high representatives, I had absolutely no interest in politics; though I did follow current events. So this would have been a few years after the Sharpeville massacre, to which I must have alluded; and doubtless my words contained some element of pious condemnation. Well, I did think it was wrong to massacre people.

"Do you even know where Sharpeville is?" The Head of the Table had evidently identified me as a mewling pinko.

"It's in South Africa," I replied. But as I did so, I suddenly wondered if this was a trick question. "Or Rhodesia," I added; then thought again. "No, South Africa."

"Very good. And what is your considered judgement on the political scene there?"

I said something about being against shooting people.

"And what might you advise the police forces of the world to do when confronted with a rioting mob of Communists?"

I hated the way adults asked you questions in a way which implied that they already knew the answer you were going to give, and that it would always be a wrong or stupid one. So I said something, perhaps facetious, to the effect that just because they were dead, this didn't prove they were Communists.

"Have you ever *been* to South Africa?" Macleod roared at me.

Susan stirred at this point. "We've none of us been to South Africa."

"True, but I think I know more about the situation there than the two of you put together." It seemed that Clara was excused from complicity in ignorance. "If we were to pile his knowledge on top of your knowledge—Pelion on Ossa, as it were—it still wouldn't amount to a hill of beans."

The long silence was broken by Susan asking if anyone wanted any more to eat.

"Have you got any beans, Mrs. Macleod?"

Yes, I could be a cheeky bastard, I now realise. Well, I was only nineteen. I hadn't a clue who or what Pelion and Ossa might be; I was more struck by the notion of piling my knowledge on top of Susan's. That was what lovers did, after all: they added to one another's understanding of the world. Also, to "know" someone, in the Bible anyway, meant to have sex with them. So I had already piled my knowledge on top of hers. Even if it didn't amount to more than a hill of beans. However tall a hill of beans might be.

She told me that her father had been a Christian Science practitioner with many adoring female acolytes. She told me that her brother who had disappeared in the war had gone to a prostitute a few weeks before his last flight because he wanted to "find out what it was all about." She told me that she couldn't swim because she had heavy bones. Things like this tumbled out of her in no particular order, and in response to no particular enquiry on my part, other than the tacit one of wanting to know everything about her. So she laid them out, as if expecting me to make sense, to make order, of her life, and of her heart.

"Things aren't what they look like, Paul. That's about the only lesson I can teach you."

I wonder if she is talking about the sham of respectability, the sham of marriage, the sham of suburbia, or . . . but she carries on.

"Winston Churchill, did I tell you about seeing him?"

"You mean, you went to Number Ten?"

"Silly, no. I saw him in a backstreet in Aylesbury. What was I doing there? Not that it matters. He was sitting in the rear seat of an open-topped car. And his face was all covered in makeup. Red lips, bright pink face. He looked bizarre."

"You're sure it was Churchill? I didn't realise he was . . ."

". . . one of them? No, it's nothing like that, Paul. You see, they were waiting to drive him through the city centre—it was after we won the war, or maybe it was the General Election, and he was made up for the cameras. Pathé News and all that."

"How weird."

"It was. So quite a few people saw this strange painted mannequin in the flesh, but far more saw him on the newsreels, when he looked like they expected him to."

I think about this for a while. It strikes me as a

comic incident, rather than a general principle of life. Anyway, my interests are elsewhere.

"But you're what you look like, aren't you? *You're* exactly what you look like?"

She kisses me. "I hope so, my fine and feathered friend. I hope so for both our sakes."

I used to prowl the Macleod house, part anthropologist, part sociologist, wholly lover. At first I naturally compared it to my parents' house, which I therefore found wanting. Here there was style, and ease, and none of that absurd house-pride. My parents had better, more up-to-date kitchen equipment, but I gave them no credit for this; nor for the fact that their car was cleaner, their gutters recently sluiced, their soffits regularly painted, their bathroom taps buffed to a shine, their lavatory seats hygienically plastic rather than warmingly wooden. In our house, the television was taken seriously, and stood centrally; at the Macleods', they called it the goggle-box and hid it behind a firescreen. They owned no such thing as a fitted carpet or a fitted kitchen, let alone a three-piece suite or a bathroom set in matching colours. Their garage was so full of tools, discarded sports equipment, gardening implements, old motor mowers (one working) and unwanted furniture that there was no room in it for the Austin. At first all this seemed stylish and idiosyncratic. I was initially seduced, then slowly disenchanted. My soul no more belonged in a place like this than in my parents' house.

And, more importantly, I believed that Susan didn't belong here either. It was something I felt instinctively, and only understood much later, over time. Nowadays, when more than half the country's children are born out of wedlock (wedlock: I've never noticed the two parts of that term before), it's not so much marriage that ties couples together as the shared occupation of property. A house or a flat can be as beguiling a trap as a wedding certificate; sometimes more so. Property announces a way of life, with a subtle insistence on that way of life continuing. Property also demands constant attention and maintenance: it's like a physical manifestation of the marriage that exists within it.

But I could see, all too well, that Susan had not been the recipient of constant attention and maintenance. And I'm not talking about sex. Or not just.

Here's something I need to explain. In all the time Susan and I were lovers, I never thought that we were "deceiving" Gordon Macleod, Mr. E.P. I never thought of him as being represented by that peculiar old word "cuckold." Obviously, I didn't want him to *know*. But I thought that what took place between Susan and me had nothing to do with him; he was irrelevant to it all. Nor did I have any contempt for him, any young-buck superiority because I was sexually active with his wife and he wasn't. You may think this is just a normal lover's normal self-delusion; but I don't agree. Even when things . . . changed, and I felt differently about him, this aspect didn't change. He had nothing to do with us, do you see?

Susan, perhaps thinking that I was undervaluing her friend Joan, had told me, in a gently admonitory tone, that everyone had their own love story. I was happy to accept this, happy for everyone else to be or have been blessed, even if confident that they couldn't possibly be as blessed as I was. But at the same time, I didn't want Susan to tell me whether she had had her love story with Gerald, or with Gordon, or was having it with me. Whether there were one, two or three stories to her life.

I am round at the Macleods' one evening. It is getting late. Macleod has already gone to bed, and is snoring away his flagons and his gallons. She and I are on the sofa; we have been listening to some music we recently heard at the Festival Hall. I look at her in a way which makes my attentions and desires plain.

"No, Casey. Kiss me hardly."

So I kiss her hardly, just a brush on the lips,

nothing to raise her colour. We hold hands instead.

"I wish I didn't have to go home," I say self-pityingly. "I hate home."

"Then why do you call it home?"

I haven't thought of this.

"Anyway, I wish I could stay here."

"You could always pitch a tent in the garden. I'm sure there's some spare tarpaulin in the garage."

"You know what I mean."

"I know exactly what you mean."

"I could always climb out of a window afterwards."

"And be arrested for burglary by a passing copper? That *would* land us in the *Advertiser & Gazette*." She paused. "I suppose . . ."

"Yes?" I hope she is coming up with a master plan.

"This thing actually turns into a sofa bed. We could put you up here. If E.P. finds you before he goes to work, we'll say—"

But just at that moment the phone rings. Susan picks it up, listens, looks at me, says, "Yes," pulls a solemn face and places her hand over the mouthpiece.

"It's for you."

It is, of course, my mother, demanding to know where I am, which I find an otiose question, given that my current address would be right next to the number in the phone book which she must have just consulted. Also, she wants to know when I shall be back.

"I'm a bit tired," I say. "So I'm staying here on the sofa bed."

My mother has recently had to put up with a certain amount of insolent lying from me; but insolent truth-telling is pushing things too far.

"You'll be doing no such thing. I'll be outside in six minutes." And then she puts the phone down.

"She'll be outside in six minutes."

"Lawks-a-mercy," says Susan. "Do you think I should offer her a glass of sherry?"

We giggle away the next five-and-three-quarter minutes until we hear a car out in the road.

"Off you go now, you dirty stop-out," she whispers.

My mother was behind the wheel in her pink dressing gown over her pink nightdress. I didn't check to see if she was driving in bedroom slippers. She was halfway down a cigarette, and before putting the car into gear, flicked the glowing stub out onto the Macleods' driveway.

I got in, and as we drove my mood switched from pert indifference to furious humiliation. An English silence—one in which all the unspoken words are perfectly understood by both parties—prevailed. I got into my bed and wept. The matter was never referred to again.

• • •

Susan's innocence was the more surprising because she never tried to hide it. I'm not sure she ever tried to hide anything—it was against her nature. Later—well, what came later, came later.

But, for instance—and I can't remember how the subject came up—she once said that she wouldn't necessarily have gone to bed with me if it hadn't been for the known fact that it was bad for a man not to have "sexual release." This is all that remains of the words spoken between us, that simple phrase.

Perhaps it was more ignorance than innocence. Or call it folk wisdom; or patriarchal propaganda. And it set me wondering. Did this mean that she didn't desire me as much as I desired her—constantly, naggingly, utterly? That sex for her meant something different? That she was only going to bed with me for therapeutic reasons, because I might explode like a hot-water cylinder or car radiator if I didn't have this necessary "release"? And was there no equivalent of this in female sexual psychology?

Later, I thought: But if that's how she imagines male sexuality to operate, what about her husband? Did she never wonder about his need for "release"? Unless, of course, she had seen him explode and so realised the consequences. Or perhaps E.P. went to prostitutes in London—

or to the front half of some pantomime elephant? Who knew? Perhaps this explained his oddity.

His oddity, her innocence. And of course I didn't tell her in reply that young men—all young men in my experience—when deprived of female company, didn't have a problem with "sexual release," for the simple reason that they are, were and always would be wanking away like jackhammers.

Her innocence, my overconfidence; her naivety, my crassness. I was going back to university. I thought it would be funny to buy her a large fat carrot as a farewell present. It would be a joke; she would laugh; she always laughed when I laughed. I went to a greengrocer's and decided a parsnip would be funnier. We went for a drive and stopped somewhere. I gave her the parsnip. She didn't laugh at all, just threw it over her shoulder, and I heard it thump against the back seat of the shooting brake. I have remembered this moment all my life, and though I haven't blushed for many years, I would blush, if I could, about that.

We managed a brief holiday. I can't remember what lies we told in order to have a few days of truth together. It must have been out of season. We went somewhere near the south coast. I can't remember a hotel, so perhaps we rented a flat.

What we said, thought, discovered about one another—all gone. I do remember a broad, empty beach somewhere. Perhaps it was Camber Sands. We photographed one another with my camera. I did handstands on the beach for her. She is wearing a coat and the wind is whipping her hair back, and her hands, holding her coat closed at the neck, are enclosed in large, black false-fur gloves. Behind her is a distant row of beach huts, and a one-storey, shuttered café. No one else is in sight. You could, if you wanted, look at these photographs and deduce the season; also, no doubt, the weather. At this distance, both are meaningless to me.

I was wearing a tie, that's another detail. I had taken off my jacket to do handstands for her. The tie falls straight down the middle of my upturned face, obscuring my nose, dividing me into two halves. Backhand and forehand.

I didn't get much post in those days. Cards from friends, letters from the university reminding me about stuff, bank statements.

"Local postmark," said my mother, handing me an envelope. The address was typed, and there was a heartening "Esq." after my name.

"Thanks, Mum."

"Aren't you going to open it?"

"I shall, Mum."

She huffed off.

The letter came from the secretary of the tennis club. He was informing me that my temporary membership had been terminated with immediate effect. Further, that "due to the circumstances," none of the membership fee I had paid was refundable. The "circumstances" were not specified.

Susan and I had arranged to meet at the club for a pick-up foursome. So after lunch I took my racket and sports bag and set off as if for the courts.

"Was the letter interesting?" my mother asked impedingly.

I waved my racket in its press.

"Tennis club. Asking if I want to join on a permanent basis."

"That's gratifying, Paul. They must be pleased with your game."

"Sounds like it, doesn't it?"

I drive to Susan's house.

"I got one too," she says.

Her letter is much the same as mine, except more strongly worded. Instead of her membership being terminated "due to the circumstances" it is terminated "due to the evident circumstances of which you will be fully aware." The adjusted wording is for Jezebels, for scarlet women.

"How long have you been a member?"

"Thirty years, I suppose. Give or take."

"I'm sorry. It's my fault."

She shakes her head in disagreement.

"Shall we protest?"

No.

"I could burn the place down."

No.

"Do you think we were spotted somewhere?"

"Stop asking questions, Paul. I'm thinking."

I sit down beside her on the chintz sofa. What I don't like to say, or not immediately, is that part of me finds the news exhilarating. I—we—are a cause of scandal! Love persecuted yet again by small-minded petty officialdom! Our expulsion might not have been an Obstacle on which Passion Thrives, but the moral and social condemnation implicit in the phrase "due to the circumstances" act, to my mind, as an authentication of our love. And who does not want their love authenticated?

"It's not as if we were caught snogging in the long grass behind the roller."

"Oh, do be quiet, Paul."

So I sit there quietly, my thoughts noisy. I try to remember cases of boys expelled from my school. One for pouring sugar into the petrol tank of a master's car. One for getting his girlfriend pregnant. One for being drunk after a cricket match, urinating in a train compartment and then pulling the communication cord. At the time, all this seemed pretty impressive stuff. But my own rule-breaking struck me as thrilling, triumphant, and, most of all, grown-up.

"Well, now look what the cat's brought in" was Joan's greeting as she answered the door a few afternoons later. I hadn't warned her of my visit. "Just give me a moment to shut up the yappers."

The door closed again, and I stood by an elderly boot scraper thinking about the distance that had grown between Susan and me since the tennis club's dismissal of us. I had let my exhilaration show too clearly, which displeased her. She said that she was still "thinking." I couldn't see what there was to think about. She told me there were complications I didn't understand. She told me not to come round until the weekend. I felt downcast, like one awaiting judgement even though no crime that I could see had been committed.

"Sit yourself down," Joan instructed as we reached the fag-fogged, gin-scented den that was nominally her sitting room. "You'll have something to put a few hairs on your chest?"

"Yes, please." I didn't drink gin—I hated the smell of it, and it made me feel even worse than wine or beer did. But I didn't want to come across as a prig.

"Good man." She handed me a tumblerful. There was a smear of lipstick at its rim.

"That's an awful lot," I said.

"We don't pour fucking pub measures in this establishment," she replied.

I sipped at the thick, oily, lukewarm substance which didn't smell at all like the juniper berries on the bottle.

Joan lit a cigarette and blew the smoke in my direction as if to nudge me.

"So?"

"So. Well. Perhaps you've heard about the tennis club."

"The Village tom-tom speaks of nothing else. The drumheads have been taking a real pasting."

"Yes, I thought you—"

"Two things, young man. One, I don't want to know any details. Two, how can I help?"

"Thank you." I was genuinely touched, but also puzzled. How could she help if she didn't know the details? And what counted as a detail? I thought about this.

"Come on. What are you here to ask me?"

That was the problem. I didn't know what I'd come to ask. I somehow thought that what I wanted from Joan would become clear to me when I saw her. Or she would know anyway. But it hadn't, and she apparently didn't. I tried to explain this, haltingly. Joan nodded, and let me sip my gin and ponder.

Then she said, "Try lobbing me the first question that comes into your head."

I did so without reflecting. "Do you think Susan would leave Mr. Macleod?"

"My, my," she said quietly. "You are aiming high, young man. That's a pair of balls you've got on you. Talk about one step at a time."

I grinned inanely at what I took to be a compliment.

"So have you asked her?"

"Gosh, no."

"And, to start at the beginning, what would you do for money?"

"I don't care about money," I replied.

"That's because you've never had to."

This was true; but not in the sense that I was rich. My state education had been free, I received a council grant to attend university, I lived at home in the holidays. But it was also true that I didn't care about money—indeed, in my world view, to care about money meant deliberately to turn your eyes away from the most important things in life.

"If you're going to be a grown-up," said Joan, "you've got to start thinking about grown-up things. And number one is money."

I remembered what I'd been told about Joan's early life—her being a "kept woman" or whatever, living no doubt from cash handouts and rent-payings and gifts of clothes and holidays. Is that what she meant by being grown-up?

"I suppose Susan's got some."

"Have you asked her?"

"Gosh, no."

"Well, maybe you should."

"I've got a running-away fund," I said defensively, without explaining where it had come from.

"And how much rattles around in your little piggy bank?"

It was odd how I never took offence at anything Joan said. I just assumed that beneath her brusqueness she was kindhearted and on my side. But then lovers always assume that people are on their side.

"Five hundred pounds," I said proudly.

"Yes, well, you could certainly run away on that. It'll keep you for a few weeks in Le Touquet–Paris–Plage as long as you don't go near the casino. And then you'll come running back to England."

"I suppose so." Even if I'd never thought of Le Touquet–Paris–Plage as a destination. Was that where fleeing lovers went?

"You're going back to college next month, aren't you?"

"Yes."

"And you're going to keep her in a kitchen cupboard there? A wardrobe?"

"No."

I felt stupid and hopeless. No wonder Susan was "thinking" about it all. Was I merely entertaining some romantic notion of flight, a ladder with no steps attached?

"It's a bit more complicated than working out how to save me on the gin and the petrol."

I had been brought solidly down to earth, as Joan no doubt intended.

"Can I ask you something different?"

"Off you go."

"Why do you cheat at crosswords?"

Joan laughed loudly. "You cheeky bugger. I suppose Susan told you. Well, it's a fair question, and one I can answer." She took another pull of her gin. "You see—I hope you never get there yourself—but some of us get to the point in life where we realise that nothing matters. Nothing fucking matters. And one of the few side benefits of that is you know you're not going to go to hell for filling in the wrong answers in the crossword. Because you've been to hell and back already and you know all too well what it's like."

"But the answers are in the back of the book."

"Ah, but you see, to me that *would* be cheating."

I felt absurdly fond of her. "Is there anything I can do for you, Joan?" I found myself asking.

"Just don't cause Susan any harm."

"I'd rather cut my own throat," I replied.

"Yes, I think you might even mean that." She smiled at me. "Now, off with you, and mind your driving. I can see you're not yet hardened to the gin."

I was about to put the car into gear when there was a tap at the window. I hadn't heard her behind me. I wound the window down.

"Don't ever care what they say about you," Joan said, looking at me intently. "For instance, some kindly neighbours assume I'm just a ghastly old lezzer living alone with my dogs. So, a failed lezzer at that. Water off a duck's back. That's my advice if you want it."

"Thank you for the gin," I replied, and released the handbrake.

Joan was demanding that I be grown-up. I was prepared to try if it helped Susan; but I still regarded adulthood with some horror. First, I wasn't sure that it was attainable. Secondly, even if attainable, I wasn't sure it was desirable. Thirdly, even if desirable, then only by comparison with childhood and adolescence. What did I dislike and distrust about adulthood? Well to put it briefly: the sense of entitlement, the sense of superiority, the assumption of knowing better if not best, the vast banality of adult opinions, the way women took out compacts and powdered their noses, the way men sat in armchairs with their legs apart and their privates heavily outlined against their trousers, the way they talked about gardens and gardening, the spectacles they wore and the spectacles they made of themselves, the drinking and the smoking, the terrible phlegmy racket when they coughed, the artificial smells they applied to conceal their animal smells, the way men went bald and women shaped their hair with aerosols of glue, the noxious thought that they might still be having sex, their docile obedience to social norms, their snarky disapproval of anything satirical or questioning, their assumption that their children's success would be measured by how well they imitated their parents, the suffocating noise they made when agreeing with one another, their comments about the food they cooked and the food they ate, their love of stuff I found disgusting (especially olives, pickled onions, chutneys, piccalilli, horseradish sauce, spring onions, sandwich spread, stinky cheese and Marmite), their emotional complacency, their sense of racial superiority, the way they counted their pennies, the way they hunted for food trapped between their teeth, the way they weren't interested enough in me, and the way they were too interested in me when I didn't want them to be. This was just a short list, from which Susan was naturally and entirely exempt.

Oh, and another thing. The way, doubtless through some atavistic terror of admitting to real feelings, they ironised the emotional life, turning the relationship between the sexes into a silly running joke. The way men implied that women ran everything really; the way women implied that men didn't really understand what was going on. The way men pretended they were the strong, and women had to be petted and indulged and taken care of; the way women pretended that, regardless of the accumulated sexual folklore, they were the ones who had the common sense and practicality. The way each sex blubbingly admitted that, for all the other's faults, they still needed one another. Can't live with 'em, can't live without 'em. And they lived with 'em in marriage, which, as one wit put it, was an institution in the sense of mental institution. Who first said that, a man or a woman?

Unsurprisingly, I looked forward to none of this. Or rather, hoped it would never apply to me; indeed, believed I could make it not apply to me.

So, actually, when I said, "I'm nineteen!" and my parents triumphantly replied, "Yes, you're *only* nineteen!" the triumph was also mine. Thank God I'm "only" nineteen, I thought.

First love fixes a life forever: this much I have discovered over the years. It may not outrank subsequent loves, but they will always be affected by its existence. It may serve as model, or as counterexample. It may overshadow subsequent loves; on the other hand, it can make them easier, better. Though sometimes, first love cauterises the heart, and all any searcher will find thereafter is scar tissue.

"We were chosen by lot." I don't believe in destiny, as I may have said. But I do believe now that when two lovers meet, there is already so much prehistory that only certain outcomes are possible. Whereas the lovers themselves imagine that the world is being reset, and that the possibilities are both new and infinite.

And first love always happens in the overwhelming first person. How can it not? Also, in the overwhelming present tense. It takes us time to realise that there are other persons, and other tenses.

So (and this would have happened earlier, but I am only remembering it now): I am visiting her one afternoon. I know that at three o'clock, by which time her thieving daily will have left and there will be three-and-a-half hours before Mr. E.P. returns, she will be waiting in bed for me. I drive to the Village, park, and set off along Duckers Lane. I am not in the least self-conscious. The more disapproval, real or imagined, from "the neighbours," the better. I do not approach the Macleod house via the back gate and the garden. I turn down their driveway, walking openly and crunching the gravel, rather than discreetly, adulterously, on the grass edge alongside. The house is red-brick, symmetrical, with a central porch, above which is Susan's narrow little bedroom. On each side of the porch, as a decorative feature, every fourth course of brick has been laid to jut out half a brick's width. A couple of tempting inches, I now see, of handhold and foothold.

The lover as cat burglar? Why not? The back door has been left open for me. But as I walk towards the porch, a lover's confidence infuses me, and I decide that if I go at it with enough initial speed, I might be able to scoot up the ten feet or so of wall, which will get me to the flat, leaded roof on top of the porch. I take a run at it, filled with bravado, ardour and decent hand-eye coordination. Easy-peasy—and here I am, suddenly crouched on the leading. I have made enough noise to bring Susan to the window, first in alarm, then in surprised glee. Someone else would have rebuked me for my folly, told me I might have broken my skull, expressed all their fear and protectiveness: in short, made me feel a foolish and guilty boy. All Susan does is yank up the window and pull me in.

"I could always get out the same way if Trouble Comes," I say pantingly.

"That would be a lark."

"I'll just go down and lock the back door."

"Ever the thoughtful one," says Susan, getting back into her single bed.

And that's true, too. I *am* the thoughtful one. That's part of my prehistory, I suppose. But it's also about what I could have said to Joan: that I am prepared to be grown-up if it will help Susan.

• • •

I am a boy; she is a married woman of middle years. I have the cynicism, and the purported understanding of life though I am the idealist as well as the cynic, convinced that I have both the will and the power to mend things.

And she? She is neither cynical nor idealistic; she lives without the mental clutter of theorising, and takes each circumstance and situation as it comes. She laughs at things, and sometimes that laughter is a way of not thinking, of avoiding obvious, painful truths. But at the same time I feel that she is closer to life than I am.

We don't talk about our love; we merely know that it is there, unarguably; that it is what it is, and that everything will flow, inevitably and justly, from this fact. Do we constantly repeat "I love you" in confirmation? At this distance, I can't be sure. Though I do remember that when, after locking the back door, I climb into bed with her, she whispers,

"Never forget, the most vulnerable spot is down the middle."

Then there's that word Joan dropped into our conversation like a concrete fence post into a fishpool: practicality. Over my life I've seen friends fail to leave their marriages, fail to continue affairs, fail even to start them sometimes, all for the same expressed reason. "It just isn't practical," they say wearily. The distances are too great, the train schedules unfavourable, the work hours mismatched; then there's the mortgage; and the children, and the dog; also, the joint ownership of things. "I just couldn't face sorting out the record collection," a non-leaving wife once told me. In the first thrill of love, the couple had amalgamated their records, throwing away duplicates. How was it feasible to unpick all that? And so she stayed; and after a while the temptation to leave passed, and the record collection breathed a sigh of relief.

Whereas it seemed to me, back then, in the absolutism of my condition, that love had nothing to do with practicality; indeed, was its polar opposite. And the fact that it showed contempt for such banal considerations was part of its glory. Love was by its very nature disruptive, cataclysmic; and if it was not, then it was not love.

You might ask how deep my understanding of love was at the age of nineteen. A court of law might find it based on a few books and films, conversations with friends, heady dreams, aching fantasies about certain girls on bicycles and a quarter-relationship with the first woman I went to bed with. But my nineteen-year-old self would correct the court: "understanding" love is for later, "understanding" love verges on practicality, "understanding" love is for when the heart has cooled. The lover, in rapture, doesn't want to "understand" love, but to experience it, to feel the intensity, the coming-into-focus of things, the acceleration of life, the entirely justifiable egotism, the lustful cockiness, the joyful rant, the calm seriousness, the hot yearning, the certainty, the simplicity, the complexity, the truth, the truth, the truth of love.

Truth and love, that was my credo. I love her, and I see the truth. It must be that simple.

Were we "any good" at sex? I've no idea. We didn't think about it. Partly because any sex then seemed by definition good sex. But also because we rarely talked about it, either before, during or after; we did it, believed in it as an expression of our mutual love, even if, physically and mentally, it might have given us different satisfactions. After she had mentioned her supposed frigidity, and I had—from my vast sexual experience—airily dismissed it, the matter was not discussed again. Sometimes, she would murmur, "Well played, partner," afterwards. Sometimes, more seriously, more anxiously, "Please don't give up on me just yet, Casey Paul." I didn't know what to say to that either.

From time to time—and not in bed, I must point out—she would say, "Of course you'll have girlfriends. And that's only right and proper." But it didn't seem right, or proper, to me, or even relevant.

On another occasion, she mentioned a number. I can't remember the context, let alone the number; but I slowly realised that she must be talking about how many times we had made love.

"You've been counting?"

She nodded. Again, I was baffled. Was I meant to have been counting too? And if so, what was I meant to count—the number of times we'd been to bed together, or the number of my orgasms? I wasn't in the least interested, and I wondered why the notion had crossed her mind. There seemed something fatalistic about it—as if she would have something tangible, calculable, to hold on to if I suddenly wasn't there. But I wasn't suddenly going to be not there.

When, once again, she made reference to my future girlfriends, I said, very clearly and firmly, that she would always be in my life: whatever happened, there would always be a place for her.

"But where would you put me, Casey Paul?"

"At the very worst, in a well-appointed attic."

I meant it metaphorically, of course.

"Like a piece of old lumber?"

I was hating this conversation. "No," I repeated, "you'll always be there."

"In your attic?"

"No, in my heart."

I meant it, I truly meant it—both the attic and the heart. All my life.

I didn't realise that there was panic inside her. How could I have guessed? I thought it was just inside me. Now, I realise, rather late in the day, that it is in everyone. It's a condition of our mortality. We have codes of manners to allay and minimise it, jokes and routines, and so many forms of diversion and distraction. But there is panic and pandemonium waiting to break out inside all of us, of this I am convinced. I've seen it roar out among the dying, as a last protest against the human condition and its chronic sadness. But it is there in the most balanced and rational of us. You just need the right circumstances, and it will surely appear. And then you are at its mercy. The panic takes some to God, others to despair, some to charitable works, others to drink, some to emotional oblivion, others to a life where they hope that nothing serious will ever trouble them again.

Though we were cast out of the tennis club like Adam and Eve, the expected scandal failed to break. There was no denunciation from the pulpit of St. Michael's, no exposure in the *Advertiser & Gazette*. Mr. Macleod seemed oblivious; Misses G. and N.S. were abroad at the time. My parents never mentioned the matter. So by a very English combination of ignorance, true or feigned, and embarrassment, no one—apart from Joan, and that at my invitation—acknowledged the story's existence. The Village tom-tom might have been beating, but not everyone chose to hear its message. I was both relieved by this and disappointed. Where was the merit, and the joy, in scandalous behaviour if the Village declined to be scandalised except behind closed doors?

But I was relieved, because it meant Susan brought her "thinking" period to an end. In other words, we took a deep breath and started going to bed together again, taking as many risks as before. I stroked her ears and tapped her rabbity teeth. Once, to demonstrate that all was still the same, I sprang up the jutting brickwork onto the porch and through her bedroom window.

And, as it turned out, she had a running-away fund too. With more than five hundred pounds in it.

I keep saying that I was nineteen. But sometimes, in what I've told you so far, I was twenty or twenty-one. These events happened over a period of two years and more, usually during my student vacations. In term time, Susan would often come and visit me in Sussex, or I would go up and stay at the Macleods'. Six minutes' drive from my parents, yet I never told them I was there. I would get off the train at a previous station, and Susan would pick me up in the Austin. I slept on the sofa bed, and Mr. Macleod seemed to tolerate my presence. I never went into the Village, though I did occasionally think of burning down the tennis club, just for old times' sake.

Susan got to know my circle of friends at Sussex—Eric, Ian, Barney and Sam—and from time to time one or more of them would also stay at the Macleods'. Perhaps they were another kind of cover story—at this distance, I can't remember. They all considered my relationship with Susan an excellent thing. We were on one another's side when it came to relationships—any relationship, really. They also liked the freewheelingness of Susan's household. She used to cook big meals, and they liked that too. We always seemed to be hungry back then; also, pathetically incapable of making a meal for ourselves.

One Friday—well, it was probably a Friday— Mr. Macleod was chomping on his spring onions, I was playing with my knife and fork and Susan was bringing in the food, when he asked, with more than the usual edge of sarcasm,

"And how many fancy boys are you providing yourself with this weekend, if I may make so bold as to ask?"

"Let me see," Susan replied, holding the stew dish in front of her as she appeared to ponder, "I think it's just Ian and Eric this weekend. And Paul of course. Unless the others turn up as well."

I thought this amazingly cool of her. And then we ate dinner normally.

But in the car the next day, I asked her, "Does he always call me that? Us that?"

"Yes. You're my fancy boy."

"I'm not *that* fancy. I'm a bit penny plain at times, I think."

But the word hurt. Hurt me for her, you understand. For myself, I didn't care. No, really: perhaps I was even pleased. To be noticed—even to be insulted—was better than to be ignored. And a young man needed a reputation, after all.

I tried to assemble what I knew about Macleod. I could no longer think of him as Mr. E.P. than I could as Old Adam or the Head of the Table. He was called Gordon, though Susan only used that name when speaking of the distant past. He looked a few years older than her, so must have been in his mid-fifties. He worked as a civil servant, though I had no idea in which department, nor was I interested. He hadn't had sex with his wife for many years, though in the old days, when he was Gordon, he had done so, and two daughters were the proof of this. He had declared his wife frigid. He might, or might not, fancy the front half of a pantomime elephant. He believed that rioting mobs of Communists should be shot by the police or army. His wife hadn't seen his eyes, or not properly, for many years. He played golf, and hit the ball as if he hated it. He liked Gilbert and Sullivan. He was good at disguising himself as a shabby but efficient gardener; though according to his own father he could be a difficult row to hoe. He didn't like or take holidays. He liked to drink. He didn't like going to concerts. He was good at crosswords and had pedantic handwriting. He didn't have any friends in the Village, except, presumably, at the golf club, a place I had never entered, and had no intention of doing so. He didn't go to church. He read *The Times* and *The Telegraph*. He had been friendly and polite with me, but also sarcastic and rude; mainly, I would say, indifferent. He seemed to be cross with life. And was part of what may or may not have been a played-out generation.

But there was another thing about him, which I felt rather than observed. It seemed to me—I'm sure Macleod wasn't conscious of it, hadn't given it a thought—but it felt to me as if he—he in particular—was somehow standing in the way of me growing up. He wasn't at all like my parents or their friends, but he represented even more than they did the adulthood I regarded with some horror.

A few stray thoughts and memories:

—Shortly after the Sharpeville Incident, Susan reported that Macleod had called me "a very acceptable young man." Desperate for praise, like anyone else of my age, I took it at face value.

Perhaps more than that: because he had first shouted at me, then later come to sober judgement, I considered the comment all the more valuable.

—I realise that I had absolutely no notion how the Macleods behaved with one another when I was not there. I was probably too absolutist to give it a thought.

—I also realise that, in comparing the two households, I might have made it sound as if at home we ate peas off a knife while scratching our bottoms. No, we were well brought-up. Our standard of table behaviour was on the whole better than that on display at the Macleods'.

—Also, not all my parents' friends were as passively disapproving of my generation as I may have portrayed them. Some were actively so. One holiday weekend, we all went over to Sutton for dinner with the Spencers. The wife had known my mother since training college days; the husband was a small, aggressive mining engineer, of Belgian origin, who specialised in locating and appropriating the mineral wealth of Africa on behalf of some international company. It must have been a sunny day (though not necessarily) because, peeking from my top pocket, was a recently acquired pair of mirrored sunglasses. I had bought them from Barney, who specialised in the bulk purchase and import of exotic items for resale to those wishing to quietly demonstrate their essential hipsterdom. He had sourced the glasses from somewhere behind the Iron Curtain—Hungary, I think. Anyway, we had scarcely got out of the car when Mine Tiny Host approached me and, ignoring my outstretched hand, ripped the sunglasses from my pocket with the words, "These are a piece of shit." Unlike, say, his own cable-knit sweater, corduroy trousers, signet ring and deaf aid.

—She makes a big cake for the Fancy Boys. Big in the sense of wide and long. When the mixture is poured into the tin, it is three-quarters of an inch deep. By the time it comes out of the oven, it has risen slightly to a height of about an inch. There is mixed fruit inside, all of which has sunk to the bottom.

Even I, back then, can recognise that it is not, by average baking standards, a success. But she has a way of making it so.

"What sort of cake is that, Mrs. Macleod?" asks one of the FBs.

"It's an upside-down cake," she replies, flipping it over on its wire rack. "Look how the fruit has all risen to the top."

Then she cuts us big slices, which we scoff.

She can probably turn base metal into gold, I think.

—I said how my credo was love and truth; I loved her, and I saw the truth. But I must also admit that this coincided with the period when I lied to my parents more often than before or since. And, to a lesser degree, to almost everybody else I knew. Though not to Joan.

—While I do not analyse my love—the whence, why, whither of it—I do sometimes try, when alone, to think about it lucidly. This is difficult; I have no previous experience, and am quite unprepared for the full engagement of heart and soul and body that being with Susan involves—the intensity of the present, the thrill of the unknown future, the discarding of all the mingy preoccupations of the past.

I lie in bed at home, trying to put feelings into words. On the one hand—and this is the part to do with the past—Jove feels like the vast and sudden easing of a lifelong frown. But simultaneously—this is the part to do with the present and the future—it feels as if the lungs of my soul have been inflated with pure oxygen. I only think like this when alone, of course. When I am with Susan, I'm not thinking what it's like to love her; I'm just being with her. And maybe that "being with her" is impossible to put into any other words.

Susan never minded my solo visits to Joan; she wasn't possessive about one of the few friends her marriage seemed to permit. I came to enjoy the mugfuls of cut-price gin; after a while, Joan allowed the yappers in, and I got used to the distraction of Yorkshire terriers grazing on my shoelaces.

"We're leaving," I told her one July afternoon.

"We? You and I? Where are we going, young Master Paul? Do you have your belongings tied up in a red-spotted handkerchief on a stick?"

I should have known she wouldn't let me get away with earnestness.

"Susan and I. We're off."

"Off where? For how long? A cruise, is it? Send me a postcard."

"There'll be lots of postcards," I promised.

It was odd, my relationship with Joan was a kind of flirting. Whereas my relationship with Susan barely had any flirting in it at all. We must have gone through all that preliminary stuff without noticing—smack into love—and so had no need for it. We had our jokes and our teases and our private phrases, of course. But I suppose it all felt—was—too serious for flirting.

"No," I said. "You know what I mean."

"Yes, I know what you mean. I've been wondering about it for some time. Given the circumstances. Half wanting it to happen, half not. But you've got guts, the pair of you, I'll say that."

I didn't think of it in terms of guts. I thought of

it in terms of inevitability. Also, doing what we both deeply wanted.

"And how is Gordon taking it all?"

"He calls me her fancy boy."

"I'm surprised he doesn't call you her fucking fancy boy."

Yes, well, probably that too.

"I shan't say I hope you know what you're doing because it's perfectly obvious neither of you has any idea what you're doing. Now, don't pull that face at me, Master Paul. No one ever does, not in your position. And I'm not going to say, Look after her, and all that stuff. I'm just going to keep my thumbs bloody hard crossed for you."

She came out to the car with me. Before getting in, I moved towards her. She raised a palm.

"No, none of that fucking huggy-huggy stuff. There's too much of it around, everyone suddenly behaving like foreigners. Be off with you before I shed a tear."

Later, I went over what she had and hadn't said to me, and wondered if she'd been spotting parallels I'd missed. No one ever knows what they're doing, not in your position. Off up to London, eh? Fancy boy, kept woman. And who's got the money? Yes, Joan was ahead of me.

Except that it wasn't going to be like that. I could hardly imagine Susan back on the Macleod doorstep in three years' time, tongue-tied, emotionally blasted, begging silently to be taken in, her life essentially over. I was confident *that* wasn't going to happen.

There was no exact Moment of Leaving, neither a surreptitious midnight skedaddle, nor some formal departure with luggage and waving hand-kerchiefs. (Who would have waved?) It was a long-drawn-out detaching, so that the moment of rupture was never clearly marked. Which didn't stop me trying to mark it, with a brief letter to my parents:

Dear Mum and Dad,
    I am moving up to London. I shall be living with Mrs. Macleod. I shall send you an address as and when.
    Yours, Paul

That seemed to cover it. I thought the "as and when" sounded properly grown-up. Well, so I was. Twenty-one. And ready to fully indulge, fully express, fully live my life. "I'm alive! I'm living!"

We were together—under the same roof, that is—for ten or more years. Afterwards, I continued to see her regularly. In later years, less often. When she died, a few years ago, I acknowledged that the most vital part of my life had finally come to a close. I shall always think of her well, I promised myself.

And this is how I would remember it all, if I could. But I can't.

TWO

Susan's running-away fund contained enough to buy a small house in Henry Road, SE15. The price was low—gentrification, and juice bars, lay far in the future. The place had been in multi-occupation: a euphemism for locks on every door, asbestos panelling, a squalid kitchenette on a half-landing, personal gas meters and personal stains in every room. Through that late summer and early autumn we stripped it all back, joyfully, the dandruff of distemper in our hair. We threw out most of the old furniture, and slept on a double mattress on the floor. We had a toaster, a kettle, and dined off takeaways from the Cypriot taverna at the end of the road.

We needed a plumber, electrician and gas man, but did the rest ourselves. I was good at rough carpentry. I made myself a desk from two broken-up chests of drawers topped with cut-down wardrobe doors; then sanded, filled and painted it until it stood, immovably heavy, at one end of my study. I cut and laid coconut matting, and tacked carpet up the stairs. Together we ripped off the parchmenty wallpaper, back to the leprous plaster, then roller-painted it in cheery, non-bourgeois colours: turquoise, daffodil, cerise. I painted my study a sombre dark green, after

Barney told me that the labour wards of hospitals were that colour, to calm expectant mothers. I hoped it might have the same effect on my own laborious hours.

I had taken to heart Joan's sceptical "And, to start at the beginning, what would you do for money?" Given that I didn't care about the stuff, I could have lived off Susan; but, given that our relationship was going to last a lifetime, I acknowledged that at some point I would have to support her rather than the other way round. Not that I knew how much money she had. I never asked about the finances of the Macleod household, nor whether Susan had a traditional Auntie Maud who would conveniently leave her all she had.

So I decided to become a solicitor. I had no exaggerated ambitions for myself; my exaggerated ambitions were all for love. But I thought of the law because I had an orderly mind, and a capacity to apply myself; and every society needs lawyers, doesn't it? I remember a woman friend once telling me her theory of marriage: that it was something you should "dip into and out of as required." This may sound dismayingly practical, even cynical, but it wasn't. She loved her husband, and "dipping out" of marriage didn't mean adultery. Rather, it was a recognition of how marriage worked for her: as a reliable ground bass to life, as something you jogged along with until such time as you needed to "dip into" it, for succour, expressions of love and the rest. I could understand this approach: there is no point demanding more than your temperament requires or provides. But as far as I understood my life at this time, I required the opposite equation. Work would be something I jogged along with; love would be my life.

I began my studies. Each morning, Susan cooked me breakfast; each evening, supper—unless I fetched us a kebab or sheftalia. Sometimes, when I arrived back, she would sing at me, "Little man, you've had a busy day." She also took my washing to the launderette and brought it home for ironing. We still went to concerts and art exhibitions. The mattress on the floor became a double bed, in which we slept together night after night, and where some of my cinematic assumptions about love and sex became subject to adjustment. For instance, the notion of lovers falling blissfully asleep in one another's arms resolved itself into the actuality of one lover falling asleep half on top of the other, and the latter, after a certain amount of cramp and interrupted circulation, gently shifting out from beneath while trying not to wake her. I also discovered that it wasn't only men who snored.

My parents didn't reply to my change-of-address letter; nor did I invite them to visit the house in Henry Road. One day I returned from college to find Susan in agitated mood. Martha Macleod, Miss Grumpy herself, had descended without warning for a tour of inspection. She was bound to have noted that whereas in the Village her mother had slept in a single bed, now she had a double one. Fortunately, in my dark green study, the sofa bed had been pulled out, and left unmade by me that morning. But then, as Susan remarked, two doubles hardly make a single. My own attitude to Martha Macleod's likely disapproval of our sleeping arrangements was—would have been—one of pride and defiance. Susan's was more complicated, though I admit I didn't spend much time on its nuances. After all, were we living together or were we not?

When she reached the two undecorated attic rooms at the top of the house, Martha had apparently said,

"You should have lodgers."

When Susan had demurred, her daughter's reply, delivered either as argument or instruction, was:

"It would be good for you."

Quite what she meant by this we debated that evening. True, there was an economic argument for lodgers: they would make the house more or less self-sufficient. But what was the moral argument? Perhaps that lodgers would give Susan something more to do than wait for the return of her shameless lover. Martha might also have intended that lodgers would somehow dilute my noxious presence, and camouflage the reality of number 23 Henry Road—of Fancy Boy Number One living brazenly with an adulteress still more than twice his age.

If Martha's visit had troubled Susan, it also, on further thought, troubled me. I had failed to consider her future relations with her daughters. My focus had all been on Macleod, on getting Susan away from him, and now, from a safe distance, divorcing him. For our joint sake, but mainly for hers. She had to scrub this mistake from her life and give herself the legal as well as the moral freedom to be happy. And being happy consisted of living with me, alone and unfettered.

It was a quiet neighbourhood, and we received few visitors. I remember one Saturday morning being stirred from the law of tort by the front doorbell. I heard Susan invite someone—two someones, a man and a woman—into the kitchen. About twenty minutes later, I heard her say, as she shut the front door,

"I'm sure you feel a whole lot better now."

"Who was that?" I asked as she passed my door. She looked in to see me.

"Missionaries," she replied. "God damn and blast them, missionaries. I let them get it all off their chests and then sent them on their way.

Better to waste their puff on me than someone they might convert."

"Not *actual* missionaries?"

"It's a general term. Actual missionaries are the worst, of course."

"You mean, these were Jehovah's Witnesses, or Plymouth Brethren, or Baptists, or something?"

"Or something. They asked me if I was worried about the state of the world. It's an obvious catch question. Then they bored on about the Bible as if I'd never heard of it. I nearly told them I knew all about it and that I was a flaming Jezebel."

And with that she left me to my studies. But instead I mused on these sudden bursts of fierce opinion, which so endeared her to me. I had been educated by books, she by life, I thought again.

One evening, the phone went. I picked it up and gave the number.

"Who is that?" said a voice I immediately recognised as Macleod's.

"Well, who's *that?*" I replied, with fake casualness.

"Gor-don Mac-leod," he said with extended heaviness. "And whom might I be having the honour of speaking to?"

"Paul Roberts."

As he banged the receiver down, I found myself wishing I'd said Mickey Mouse, or Yuri Gagarin, or the chairman of the BBC.

I didn't tell Susan about this. I didn't see the point.

But a few weeks later we received a visit from a man called Maurice. Susan had met him before, once or twice. He might have had a connection to Macleod's office. There must have been some arrangement made. It seemed he had picked a time when I would be there too. I'm not sure about it all, at this distance—maybe it was just luck on his part.

I failed to ask any of the obvious questions at the time. And if I had, perhaps Susan would have had the answers, perhaps not.

He was a man of fiftyish, I suppose. In my memory I have given him—or he has acquired over the years—a trench coat, and perhaps a broad-brimmed hat, underneath which he wore a suit and tie. He was perfectly cordial in behaviour. He shook my hand. He accepted a cup of coffee, he used the lavatory, he asked for an ashtray, and he talked about the bland, general topics adults went in for. Susan was in her hostess mode, which involved tamping down some of the things I most loved her for: her irreverence, her free-spirited laughter at the world.

All I can remember is that at one point the conversation turned to the closure of *Reynolds News*. This was a paper—*Reynolds News and Sunday Citizen*, to give its full title—which had fallen on hard times, relaunched itself as a tabloid Sunday, and then finally closed—presumably not long before this conversation.

"I don't think it matters much," I said. I didn't really have any view on the matter. I might have seen a copy or two of *Reynolds News*, but was mainly just reacting to Maurice's tone of deep concern.

"You don't?" he asked civilly.

"No, not really."

"What about the diversity of the press? Isn't that something to be valued?"

"All the papers seem much the same to me, so I don't see that one fewer of them matters much."

"Are you by any chance part of the Revolutionary Left?"

I laughed at him. Not at his words, but at him. What the fuck did he take me for? Or perhaps, Who the fuck? He might as well have been a member of the tennis club committee, back at the Village.

"No, I despise politics," I said.

"You despise politics? Do you think that's an entirely healthy attitude? Do you find cynicism a comfortable position? What would you replace them with? You'd close down newspapers, you'd close down our way of doing politics? You'd close down democracy? That sounds like a Revolutionary Left position to me."

Now the fellow was really annoying me. I

wasn't out of my area of competence so much as my area of interest.

"I'm sorry," I said. "It's really not that at all. But you see," I added, looking at him with melancholy seriousness, "it's just that I'm a member of a played-out generation. You may think we're a bit young for it, but even so, we're played out."

He left shortly afterwards.

"Oh, Casey Paul, you are one wicked person."

"Me?"

"You. Didn't you hear him say he'd worked for *Reynolds News*?"

"No, I thought he was a spy."

"You mean, a Russki?"

"No, I just mean he was sent along to check up on us and report back."

"Probably."

"Do you think we should worry about that?"

"Not for a couple of days at least, I'd say."

You decide that, since you are a student, and all your fellow students, apart from those who live at home, pay rent, then you should do so too. You ask a couple of friends how much they pay. You take the midpoint: four pounds a week. You can afford this out of your state grant.

One Monday evening, you hand Susan four pound notes.

"What's that?" she asks.

"I've decided I should pay you rent," you reply, perhaps a little stiffly. "That's about what others pay."

She throws the notes back at you. They don't hit your face, as they might do in a film. They just lie on the floor between you. Awkward silences follow, and you sleep on your sofa bed that night. You feel guilty about not having introduced the subject of rent with more subtlety; it was like when you gave her that parsnip. The four green pound notes lie on the floor all night. The next morning you pick them up and put them back in your wallet. The subject is never mentioned again.

As a result of Martha's visit, two things happened. The attic rooms were let out to lodgers, and Susan went back to the Village for the first time since we ran away together. She said it would be necessary and practical to return from time to time. Half the house belonged to her, and she could hardly rely on Macleod to pay the bills or remember to get the boiler serviced. (I didn't see why not, but still.) Mrs. Dyer would continue to serve and thieve on a daily basis, and would alert Susan to anything that needed her attention. She promised that she would only go back when Macleod wasn't there. Grudgingly, I agreed.

I said a bit ago that "This is how I would remember it all, if I could. But I can't." There's some stuff I left out, stuff I can't put off any longer. Where to start? In the "book room," as they called it, downstairs at the Macleods'. It was late, and I was unwilling to go home. Susan might already have been in bed; I don't remember. Nor do I remember what book I was reading. Something I'd picked off the shelves at random, no doubt. I was still trying to get my head round the Macleod collection. There were leather-bound sets of the classics, old enough to have been handed down through maybe two generations; art monographs, poetry, a lot of history, some biography, novels, thrillers. I came from the sort of household where books, as if to confirm that they should be respected, were put in order: by subject, author, even size. Here, there was a different system—or rather, as far as I could see, no system at all. Herodotus was next to *The Bab Ballads*, a three-volume history of the Crusades next to Jane Austen, T. E. Lawrence sandwiched between Hemingway and a Charles Atlas manual of bodybuilding. Was it all an elaborate joke? Mere bohemian muddle? Or a way of saying: we control the books, they don't control us.

I was still musing when the door banged back against the bookcase, then rebounded far enough to be kicked again. Macleod stood there in his dressing gown, which—and this I do remember—was plaid, with a maroon cord tied and dangling.

Below were his elephant pyjamas and leather slippers.

"What are you doing here?" he asked, in a tone of voice normally attached to the words "Fuck off."

My default position of insolence kicked in.

"Reading," I replied, waving the book in his direction.

He stomped across and ripped it from my hand, briefly inspected it, then threw it like a Frisbee across the room.

I couldn't help grinning. He thought he was chucking my book away, when it was one of his own. Hilarious!

That was when he hit me. Or rather, aimed a succession of blows—three, I'm pretty sure—one of which landed as a wrist slapping the side of my head. The other two flailed past.

I got up and tried to hit him back. I think I aimed one blow, which skidded off his shoulder. Neither of us was doing any snappy defensive work; we were just equally incompetent attackers. Well, I'd never hit anyone before. He, I assume, had, or had at least tried to.

While he was concentrating on what to say, or where to hit, next, I squirmed past him, ran to the back door, and escaped. I was relieved to get back to a house where I hadn't been assaulted since a few doubtless-merited spankings a decade and more previously.

• • •

No, that wasn't quite true—about never having hit someone. In my first year at school, the gym master had encouraged us all to enter the annual boxing competition, which was organised by weight and age. I had absolutely no desire to inflict or receive pain. But I noticed that, with only a few hours to go, there were no entrants listed under my category. So I gave my name in, expecting to win by walkover.

Unfortunately for me—for both of us— another boy, Bates, had the same idea at almost the same time. So we found ourselves in the ring together, two skinny, scared things in plimsolls, vests and house shorts, with these big bobbly gloves suddenly at the end of our arms. For a couple of minutes we each did a reasonably good job of feinting attacks and then backpedalling at great speed, until the gym master pointed out that neither of us had yet landed a blow.

"Box!" he had commanded.

Whereupon I leaped at the unprepared Bates, whose gloves were down near his knees, and punched him on the nose. He squealed, looked at the sudden blood on his clean white vest and burst into tears.

And so I became school boxing champion in the under-12, under-6-stone category. Naturally, I never fought again.

• • •

The next time I went to the Macleod house, Susan's husband couldn't have been friendlier. Perhaps that was when he showed me how to do the crossword, making it some kind of exclusive male preserve. Or at any rate, a Susan-excluding one. So I put the book-room incident down as an aberration. And anyway, it might have been partly my fault. Perhaps I should have engaged him about which version of the Dewey system his library was organised under. No, I can see that might have been equally provoking.

How much time then went by? Let's call it six months. Again, it was lateish. At the Macleod house, unlike my own, there was a main staircase near the front door, and a narrower one near the kitchen, presumably for those mob-capped servants now replaced by machines. Often, when I visited Susan during term time, I would sleep in a small attic room which could be reached from either direction. Susan and I had been listening to the gramophone—preparing for a concert—and the music was still in my head when I reached the top of the back stairs. All of a sudden there came a kind of roar, and something which might have been a kick or a trip, accompanied by a thump on the shoulder, and I found myself falling back down the stairs. I managed somehow to grab the banister, wrenching my shoulder but just about keeping my balance.

"You fucking bastard!" I said automatically.

"Whatski?" came an answering bellow from above. "Whatski, my fine and feathered friend?"

I looked up at the squat bully glaring down at me from the semi-darkness. I thought that Macleod must be absolutely, certifiably mad. We stared at one another for a few seconds, then the dressing-gowned figure stomped away, and I heard a distant door close.

It wasn't Macleod's fists I was afraid of—not principally. It was his anger. We didn't do anger in my family. We did ironic comment, snappy rejoinder, satirical elaboration; we did exact words forbidding a certain action, and more severe ones condemning what had already taken place. But for anything beyond this, we did the thing enjoined upon the English middle classes for generations. We internalised our rage, our anger, our contempt. We spoke words under our breath. We might have written some of those words down in private diaries if we kept them. But we also thought that we were the only ones reacting like this, and it was a little shameful, and so we internalised it all even further.

When I got to my room that night, I placed a chair at an angle, wedged under the doorknob, as I'd seen done in films. I lay in bed thinking: Is this what the adult world is really like? Underneath it all? And how close beneath the surface does it—will it—lie?

I had no answers.

. . .

I didn't tell Susan about either of these incidents. I internalised my anger and shame—well, I would, wouldn't I?

And you'll have to imagine long spells of happiness, of delight, of laughter. I've described them already. That's the thing about memory, it's . . . well, let me put it like this. Have you ever seen an electric log-splitter in action? They're very impressive. You cue the log to a certain length, lay it on the bed of the machine, press the button with your foot, and the log is pushed onto a blade shaped like an ax-head. Whereupon the log splits pure and straight down the grain. That's the point I'm trying to make. Life is a cross section, memory is a split down the grain, and memory follows it all the way to the end.

So I can't not continue. Even if this is the hardest part to remember. No, not to remember—to describe. It was the moment when I lost some of my innocence. That may sound like a good thing. Isn't growing up a necessary process of losing one's innocence? Maybe, maybe not. But the trouble with life is, you rarely know when that loss is going to happen, do you? And how it will be, afterwards.

My parents were away on holiday, and my granny—my mother's mother—had been drafted in to look after me. I was, of course, twenty—*only* twenty—so obviously couldn't be left in the house by myself. What might I get up to, whom might I import, what might I organise—a bacchanalia of middle-aged women, perhaps— what might the neighbours think, and who might subsequently refuse to come for sherry? Grandma, widowed some five years, didn't have anything better to do. I had naturally— innocently—loved her as a child. Now I was growing up and she seemed boring. But that was a loss of innocence I could handle.

At this time, I used to sleep quite late during the holidays. It could have been mere idleness, or a belated reaction to the stress of the university term; or, perhaps, some instinctive unwillingness to reenter this world I still called home. I would sleep on until eleven without compunction. And my parents—to their credit—never came in and sat on my bed and complained that I was treating the place like a hotel; while Grandma was happy to cook me breakfast at lunchtime if that's what I wanted.

So it was probably closer to eleven than ten when I stumbled downstairs.

"There's a very rude woman asking for you," said Grandma. "She's rung three times. She told me to wake you up. Actually, the last time to 'B' wake you up. I said I'm not interfering with his beauty sleep."

"Good for you, Grandma. Thanks."

A very rude woman. But I didn't know any.

Someone from the tennis club, persecuting me further? The bank about my overdraft? Maybe Grandma was beginning to lose her marbles. At which point, the phone went again.

"Joan," said the very rude voice of Joan. "It's Susan. Get over there. She wants you, not me. *You, now.*" And she put the phone down.

"Aren't you having your breakfast?" asked Grandma as I rushed out.

At the Macleods', the front door was open, and I walked around until I found her fully dressed, handbag beside her, on the sofa in the sitting room. She didn't look up when I greeted her. I could only see the top of her head, or rather, the curve of her headscarf. I sat down beside her, but she immediately turned her face away.

"I need you to drive me up to town."

"Of course, darling."

"And I need you not to ask me any questions. And absolutely not to look at me."

"Whatever you say. But you'll need to tell me roughly where we're going."

"Head for Selfridges."

"Are we in a hurry?" I allowed myself that question.

"Just drive safely, Paul, just drive safely."

We got to near Selfridges and she directed me down Wigmore Street, then left up one of those streets where private doctors practise.

"Park here."

"Do you want me to come with you?"

"I'd rather not. Get yourself some lunch. This won't be quick. Do you need some money?"

I had indeed come without my wallet. She gave me a ten-shilling note.

As I turned back into Wigmore Street, I saw ahead of me John Bell & Croyden, where she had gone for her Dutch cap. A terrible realization came upon me. That the system had failed, that she'd found herself pregnant, and was even now dealing with the consequences. The Abortion Law was still going through Parliament, but everyone knew there were doctors—and not just at the backstreet end—who would perform "procedures" more or less on demand. I imagined the conversation: Susan explaining how she had got herself pregnant by her young lover, hadn't had sex with her husband for two decades, and how a child would destroy her marriage and endanger her own mental health. That would be enough for any doctor, who would agree to what went down euphemistically in medical records as a D&C: dilatation and curettage. Just a little scraping away at the lining of the womb—which would also scrape away the embryo attached to its wall.

I was working all this out as I sat in an Italian café having my lunch. I didn't know what I thought—or rather, I thought several incompatible things. The notion of being a father while still a student struck me as terrifying and crazy. But it also struck me as, well, kind of heroic. Subversive yet honourable, annoying yet life-affirming: noble. I didn't think it would get me into the *Guinness Book of Records*—no doubt there were twelve-year-olds hard at work getting their grannies' best friends pregnant, but it would certainly make me exceptional. And irritate the hell out of the Village.

Except that now it wasn't going to happen. Because Susan was getting rid of our child at this very moment, just around the corner. I felt sudden rage. A woman's right to choose—yes, I believed in that, theoretically and actually. Though I also believed in a man's right to be consulted.

I went back to the car and waited. After an hour or so she turned the corner and came towards me, head lowered, scarf pulled around her cheeks. She averted her face from me as she got into the car.

"Right," she said. "That's that for the moment." There was something slurry about her articulation. The anaesthetic, presumably—if they used any. "Home, James, and don't spare the horses."

Normally I was charmed by her turns of phrase. Not this time.

"First tell me where you've been."

"The dentist."

"The dentist?" So much for my imaginings.

Unless this was just another euphemism among women of Susan's class.

"I'll tell you when I can, Casey Paul. I can't tell you now. Don't ask."

Of course not. I drove her home, as carefully as I could.

Over the next days, she told me bit by bit what had happened. She had been sitting up late, listening to the gramophone. Macleod had gone to bed an hour previously. She kept playing over and over again the slow movement of Prokofiev's third piano concerto, which we'd heard a few days before at the Festival Hall. Then she put the record back in its sleeve and went upstairs. She was just reaching for the handle of her bedroom door when her hair was seized from behind, and with the words, "How's your fucking musical education coming along?," her husband smashed her face into the closed door. Then he had gone back to bed.

The dentist's examination showed that her two front teeth were broken beyond repair. The two teeth on either side of them would probably have to go as well. There was a crack in her upper jaw which would, over time, heal itself. The dentist would make her a plate. He asked if she wanted to talk about how it had happened, but didn't press her when she said she would rather not.

As the bruising came up in all its furious colours, and she powdered over it as well as she

145

could; as I drove her up to town and back for appointment after appointment; as I wasn't able to get her to look at me for days, or kiss me for weeks; as I realised I would never again be able to tap her "rabbit teeth," long discarded in some Wimpole Street waste bin; as I understood that I now had greater responsibilities than before; as I found myself wondering, and not idly, how I might kill Gordon Macleod; as first my grandma and then my returning parents drove me mad with their careful, safe, banal views of life; as Susan's bravery and lack of self-pity nearly broke my heart; as I absented myself from her house a good hour before Macleod's daily return; as I accepted her word—or was it his word?—that nothing like this would ever happen again; as anger and pity and horror washed through me; as I realised that Susan would have to leave the bastard somehow, with me or without me, but obviously with me; as at the same time a kind of impotence overcame me; as all this was happening, I learned a little more about the Macleod marriage.

Of course, that bruise on her upper arm had not just been the size of a thumbprint, it was the imprint of an actual thumb as he forced her to sit in a chair and listen to his denunciations. There had been grabbings and slappings, and more than a punch or two. He would put a glass of sherry down in front of her and order her to "join in the fun." When she declined, he would grasp her by the hair, pull her head back and hold the glass to her lips. Either she drank, or he poured it down her chin, and throat and dress. It was all verbal and physical, never sexual; though whether there was anything sexual behind it . . . well, that is beyond my competence, or, indeed, interest. Yes, it was usually connected to his drinking, but not necessarily; yes, she was frightened of him, except that mostly she wasn't. She had learned to manage him over the years. Yes, every time he attacked her, it was of course her fault— according to him; she drove him to it with her airy bloody insolence—that had been one of his phrases. Also, her irresponsibility; also, her stupidity. At some point after he had smashed her face against the door, he had gone downstairs and bent Prokofiev's third piano concerto until the record broke.

It was, I suppose, ignorance and snobbery on my part which had hitherto made me assume that domestic violence was confined to the lower classes, where things were done differently, where—as I understood from my reading rather than from a close familiarity with backstreet life—women would rather their husbands hit them than be unfaithful to them. If he beats you, it shows he loves you, and all that crap. The idea of violence being inflicted by husbands with a Cambridge degree seemed to me incomprehensible. Of course, it was not a matter I'd had reason to think about before. But if I had, I would probably have guessed that violence among working-class husbands was connected to inarticulacy: they fell back on their fists whereas middle-class husbands fell back on words. Both these myths took some years to dispel, despite the present evidence.

Susan's dental plate caused her constant trouble; there were many drives up to town for adjustments. The dentist had also made the four new prosthetic teeth better aligned than the original ones, and shortened the central pair by a millimetre or two. A subtle change, but one always manifest to me. Those teeth I used to tap so lovingly were gone forever; and I had no desire to touch their replacements.

One thing I never swerved from was the certainty that Gordon Macleod's behaviour was a crime of absolute liability. And his responsibility was also absolute. A man hits a woman; a husband hits a wife; a drunkard hits a sober spouse. There was no defence, and no possible mitigation. The fact that it would never come to court, that middle-class England had a thousand ways of avoiding the truth, that respectability was no more shed in public than clothes, the fact that Susan would never accuse him to any authority, not even a dentist—all this had no relevance to me, except sociologically. The man was as guilty as hell, and I would hate him until the end of his days. This much I knew.

It was about a year after this that I went to see Joan and announced our intention of moving up to London.

You are an absolutist for love, and therefore an absolutist against marriage. You have given the matter much thought, and come up with many fanciful comparisons. Marriage is a dog kennel in which complacency lives and is never chained up. Marriage is a jewellery box which, by some mysterious opposite of alchemy, turns gold, silver and diamonds back into base metal, paste and quartz. Marriage is a disused boathouse containing an old, two-person canoe, no longer water-worthy, with holes in the bottom and one missing paddle. Marriage is . . . oh, you have dozens of such comparisons to hand.

You remember your parents, and your parents' friends. They were, on the whole, and without giving them too much credit, decent people: honest, hardworking, polite with one another, no more than averagely controlling of their children. Family life meant for them much what it had meant for their parents' generation, though with just enough extra social freedom to let them imagine themselves pioneers. But where was love in all of this, you asked. And you didn't even mean sex— because you preferred not to think about that.

And so, when you had come into the Macleod household, and inspected a different way of living, you thought first about how circumscribed your own home seemed to be, how lacking in life and emotion. Then, gradually, you realised that the marriage of Gordon and Susan Macleod was, in fact, in far worse shape than any marriage among your parents' circle, and you became all the more absolutist. That Susan should live with you in a state of love was obvious; that she should leave Macleod was equally obvious; that she should divorce him—especially after what he had done to her—seemed not just an acknowledgement of the truth of things, not just a romantic obligation, but a necessary first step towards her becoming an authentic person once more. No, not "once more": really, it would be for the first time. And how exciting must that be for her?

You persuade her to see a solicitor. No, she doesn't want you to come with her. Part of you— the part that imagines a free, and freestanding, Susan in the near future—approves.

"How did it go?"

"He said that I was in a bit of a muddle."

"He said *that?*"

"No. Not exactly. But I explained things to him. Most things. Not you, obviously. And, well, I suppose he thought I'd just bolted. Done a bunk. Maybe he thought it was all to do with the Dreaded."

"But . . . didn't you explain what had happened . . . what *he* did to you?"

"I didn't go into detail, no. I kept it general."

"But you can't get a divorce on *general* grounds. You can only get a divorce on particular grounds."

"Now don't get shirty with me, Paul, I'm doing my best."

"Yes, but . . ."

"He told me that, for a starting point, I should go away and write it all down. Because he could see I found it hard to tell him about it directly."

"That sounds very sensible." Suddenly, you approve of this solicitor.

"So that's what I shall try to do."

When, a couple of weeks later, you ask how her statement is coming along, she shakes her head without reply.

"But you've got to do it," you say.

"You don't know how hard it is for me."

"Would you like me to help you?"

"No, I have to do this by myself."

You approve. This will be the start, the making, of the new Susan. You try some gentle advice.

"I think what they need are specifics." You know a bit about divorce law by now. "Exactly what happened, and roughly when."

Another two weeks later, you ask how she's doing.

"Don't give up on me just yet, Casey Paul" is

her reply. And whenever she says this to you—and you never think it is calculated, because she is not a calculating person—it tears at your heart. Of course you won't give up on her.

And then, some weeks later, she gives you a few sheets of paper.

"Don't read it in front of me."

You take it away, and from the first sentence, your optimism disperses. She has turned her life, and her marriage, into a comic short story, which sounds to you like something by James Thurber. Perhaps it was. It is about a man in a three-piece suit, called Mr. Elephant Pants, who every evening goes to the pub—or the bar at Grand Central Station—and comes home in a state which alarms his wife and children. He knocks over the hatstand, kicks the flowerpots, shouts at the dog, so that there is a spreading of Great Alarm and Despondency, and he rackets away until he falls asleep on the sofa and snores so loudly that tiles fall off the roof.

You don't know what to say. You say nothing. You pretend you are still considering this document. You know you have to be very gentle and very patient with her. You explain again about them needing to know specifics, the where and the when and, most importantly, the what. She looks at you and nods.

Slowly, over the next weeks and months, you begin to understand that it is not going to happen, not ever. She is strong enough to love you, strong enough to run off with you, but not strong enough to enter a court of law and give evidence against her husband about the decades of sexless tyranny, alcoholism and physical attack. She will not be able—even via her solicitor—to ask the dentist to describe her injuries. She cannot attest in public to what she is able to admit in private.

You realise that, even if she is the free spirit you imagined her to be, she is also a damaged free spirit. You understand that there is a question of shame at the bottom of it. Personal shame; and social shame. She may not mind being thrown out of the tennis club for being a Scarlet Woman, but she cannot admit to the true nature of her marriage. You remember old cases in which criminals—even murderers—would marry their female accomplices because a wife could not be compelled to give evidence against a husband. But nowadays, far away from the world of criminality, in the respectable Village and many, many similar, silent places across the land, there are wives who have been conditioned, by social and marital convention, not to give evidence against their husbands.

And there is another factor, of which, strangely, you have not thought. One calm evening—calm because you have officially given up on the project, and all false hope and annoyance have drained from you—she says to you quietly,

"And anyway, if I did do it, he'd bring up the matter of you."

You are astounded. You feel you had nothing to do with the breakup of the Macleod marriage; you were just the outsider who pointed out what would have been obvious to anyone. Yes, you fell in love with her; yes, you ran away with her; but that was consequence, not cause.

Even so, perhaps you are lucky that the old law of enticement is no longer on the statute book. You imagine being called as a witness and asked to explain yourself. Part of you thinks this would be wonderful, heroic; you play through the courtroom exchange, in which you are dazzling. Until the final question. Oh, and by the way, young enticer, young seducer, may I ask what you do by way of a job? Of course, you reply, I am studying to be a solicitor. You realise that you might just have to change profession.

You know that sometimes, after checking on the house she owns half of, she goes to visit Joan. This is a good idea, even if on her return her hair smells of cigarette smoke. Once, you catch sherry on her breath.

"Did you have a drink with Joan?"

"Did I? Let me think . . . Quite possibly."

"Well, you shouldn't. Drink and drive. It's crazy."

"Yes, sir," she agrees satirically.

Another time, she has smoke in her hair and Polos on her breath. You think, This is silly.

"Look, if you're going to have a drink with Joan, don't insult my intelligence by chewing a few Polos afterwards."

"The thing is, Paul, there are parts of the drive I don't like. They give me the jitters. Blind corners. I find that a little nip of sherry with Joan calms my nerves. And the Polos aren't for you, darling, they're in case I get stopped by a policeman."

"I'm sure policemen are just as suspicious of drivers smelling of Polos as when they smell of alcohol."

"Don't *you* turn into a policeman, Paul. Or a lawyer, even if you are going to be one. I'm doing my best. That's all I can do."

"Of course."

You kiss her. You have no more taste for confrontation than she does. Of course you trust her, of course you love her, of course you are far too young to be a policeman or a lawyer.

And so you both laugh your way through several uncomplicated months.

But one February afternoon, she is late back from the Village. You know she doesn't like driving in the dark. You imagine the car off the road, in a ditch, her bloodied head against the dashboard, Polos spilling from her handbag.

You ring Joan.

"I'm a bit worried about Susan."

"Why?"

"Well, what time did she leave you?"

"When?"

"Today."

"I haven't seen Susan today." Joan's voice is steady. "I wasn't expecting her either."

"Oh fuck," you say.

"Let me know when she's back safely."

"Sure," you say, your mind only half there.

"And Paul."

"Yes?"

"If she comes back safely, that's the main thing."

"Yes."

It is the main thing. And she does come back safely. And her hair is clean, and there is nothing on her breath.

"Sorry I'm late, darling," she says, putting down her handbag.

"Yes, I was worrying."

"No need to worry."

"Well I do."

You leave it at that. After supper, you pick up the plates, and, making sure your back is to her, ask,

"How's old Joan?"

"Joan? Same as ever. Joan doesn't change. That's what's nice about her."

You rinse off the plates and leave it at that. You are a lover, not a lawyer, you remind yourself. Except that you are going to become a lawyer, because you need to be solid and stable, the better to look after her.

The log of memory splits down the grain. So you can't remember the quiet times, the outings, the jollity, the running jokes, even the legal studies, which fill the gap between that last exchange and the day when, worried by a succession of late returns from the Village, you say to her, quietly and unchallengingly,

"I know you don't always go and see Joan when you say you do."

She looks away.

"Have you been checking up on me, Casey Paul? It's a terrible unloving thing to do, check up on people."

"Yes, but I can't stop worrying, and I can't bear to think of you alone in the house with . . . him."

"Oh, I'm quite safe," she says. There is a silence for a while. "Look, Paul, I don't tell you about it because I don't want the two parts of my life overlapping. I want to build a wall around us here."

"But?"

"But there are practical matters to discuss with him."

"Like divorce?"

Immediately, you feel ashamed of your sarcasm.

"Don't badger me like that, Mr. Badger. I've

got to do things in my own time. It's all more complicated than you think."

"OK."

"We—he and I—have two children together, don't forget that."

"I don't." Though of course, you do. Often.

"There's money to discuss. The car. The house. I think the place needs repainting this summer."

"You discuss painting the house?"

"That's enough from you, Mr. Badger."

"OK," you say. "But you love me and you don't love him."

"You know that's how it is, Casey Paul. I wouldn't be here if it wasn't."

"And I suppose *he* would like you to return."

"What I *hate*," she says, "is when he gets down on his knees."

"He gets down on his knees?" In his elephant pants, I think.

"Yes, it's awful, it's embarrassing, it's undignified."

"And, what, begs you to stay with him?"

"Yes. You see why I don't tell you about it?"

The Fancy Boys used to turn up at Henry Road and sleep on the floor, dossing like dogs on piles of cushions. The more of them there were, the more busily relaxed Susan became. So this was all good. Sometimes they brought their girlfriends, whose reactions to Henry Road used to intrigue me. I became expert in sensing covert disapproval. I wasn't being defensive or paranoid, merely observant. Also, I was amused by the orthodoxy of their sexual outlook. You might have thought—mightn't you?—that a girl or young woman in her early twenties would be rather encouraged by the notion that something exciting might happen to her nearly three decades on: that her heart and body would still be excitable, and that her future didn't necessarily have to be a matter of rising social acceptance combined with slow emotional diminution. I was surprised that some of them didn't find my relationship with Susan a cause for cheer. Instead, they reacted much as their parents would have done: alarmed, threatened, moralistic. Perhaps they were looking forward to being mothers themselves, and imagining their precious sons being cradle-snatched. Anyone would have thought Susan was a witch who had entranced me, fit only for the ducking stool. Well, she had entranced me. And to feel the disapproval from women of my own age merely increased my pleasure at Susan's and my originality, and my own determination to continue offending the prim and the unimaginative. Well, we all have to have a purpose in life, don't we? Just as a young man needs a reputation.

Around this time, one of the lodgers moved out, and Eric, having broken up with his (moralistic, marriage-demanding) girlfriend, took over the free room on the top floor. This brought a new dynamic to the house, perhaps even a better one. Eric thoroughly approved of our relationship, and would be able to keep an eye on Susan when I couldn't. He was allowed to pay rent, which made it seem the more illogical that Susan wouldn't take any from me. But I knew how she would react if I renewed my offer.

A few months passed. One evening, after Susan had gone to bed, Eric said,

"Don't like to mention this . . ."

"Yes?"

He looked embarrassed, which was unlike Eric.

". . . but the thing is, Susan's been nicking my whisky."

"Your whisky? She doesn't even drink whisky."

"Well, it's her, or you, or the poltergeist."

"You're sure?"

"I put a mark on the bottle."

"How long's this been going on?"

"A few weeks. Maybe months?"

"*Months?* Why didn't you tell me?"

"Wanted to make sure. And she changed her tactics."

"How do you mean?"

"Well, at some point she must have noticed that there was a mark on the bottle. She'd have her nip or glug or however much it was, and then fill the bottle back up to the mark with water."

"That's clever."

"No, it's standard. Banal, even. My dad used to do that when my mum was trying to get him to stop."

"Oh." I was disappointed. I wanted Susan always to be as entirely original as she still appeared to me.

"So I did the logical thing. I stopped drinking from the bottle myself. She'd come up, have a swig, fill up to the pencil mark with water. I let it run and run, until I could see the colour of the whisky fading. Eventually, to confirm it, I had a glass myself. One part whisky to about fifteen of water would be my guess."

"Fuck."

"Yes, fuck."

"I'll have a word with her," I promised.

But I didn't. Was it cowardice, the hope that some alternative explanation might present itself, or a weary refusal to admit my own suspicions?

"And in the meantime, I'll keep my booze on top of the wardrobe."

"Good plan."

It was a good plan, until the day when Eric said quietly,

"She's learned to climb up to the top of the wardrobe."

He made it sound like a kind of monkey trick rather than a normal piece of behaviour involving a chair. But that's how it felt to me too.

. . .

You notice there are times when she seems, not squiffy, but out of focus. Not bleary of face, but bleary of mind. Then, by chance, you notice her swallowing a pill.

"Headache?"

"No," she replies. She is in one of those moods—lucid, unselfpitying, yet somehow beaten-down—which bend your heart painfully. She comes and sits on the edge of the bed.

"I went to the doctor. I explained what had happened. I explained that I'd been feeling depressed. He gave me some cheering-up pills."

"I'm sorry you need them. I must be letting you down."

"It's not you, Paul. And it's not fair on you either. But I think if I can get through the . . . adjustment, then it'll get better."

"Did you tell him you were drinking a bit too much?"

"He didn't ask about that."

"That doesn't mean you shouldn't have told him."

"We're not going to quarrel about this, are we?"

"No. We're not going to quarrel. Ever."

"Then it'll all come out right. You'll see."

Thinking about this conversation later, you begin to understand—for the first time, really—that she has more to lose than you. Much more.

You are leaving behind a past, much of which you are happy to let go. You believed, and still believe as deeply, that love is the only thing that counts; that it makes up for everything; that if you and she get it right, everything will fall into place. You realise that what she has left behind— even her relationship with Gordon Macleod—is more complicated than you had assumed. You thought chunks could be cleanly amputated from a life without pain or complication. You realise that, if she had seemed isolated in the Village when you first met her, you have made her more isolated by taking her away.

All this means that you must redouble your commitment to her. You must get through this tricky patch, and then things will become clearer, better. She believes that, and so you must believe it too.

You take the back route as you approach the Village, to avoid passing your parents' house.

"Where's Susan?" are Joan's first words as she opens the door.

"I've come by myself."

"Does she know?"

You like the way Joan always gets straight to the point. You quite enjoy having cold water dashed in your face before sitting down with a streaky tumbler full of room-temperature gin.

"No."

"Then it must be serious. I'll shut the little yappers up."

You sink into a dog-scented armchair and a drink is put next to you. As you are gathering your thoughts, Joan gets in first.

"Point One. I'm not a go-between. Whatever you say stays in this room and it doesn't get leaked back. Point Two. I'm not a shrink, I'm not some kind of advice centre, I don't even much like listening to other people's woes. I tend to think they should get on with it, stop moaning, roll up their sleeves and all of that. Point Three. I'm just an old soak whose life hasn't worked out and who lives alone with her dogs. So I'm not an authority on anything. Not even crosswords, as you once pointed out."

"But you love Susan."

"Course I do. How is the dear girl?"

"She's drinking too much."

"How much is 'too much'?"

"In her case, anything at all."

"You may be right."

"And she's on antidepressants."

"Well, we've all been *there*," says Joan. "Doctors hand them out like Smarties. Especially to women of a certain age. Do they do any good?"

"I can't tell. They just make her woozy. But a different kind of woozy from what the drink does."

"Yes, I remember that too."

"So?"

"So what?"

"So what should I do?"

"Paul, dear, I've just told you I don't give advice. I took my own advice for so many years and look where it got me. So I don't do that anymore."

You nod. You aren't too surprised either.

"The only advice I'd give you . . ."

"Yes?"

". . . is have a swig of what's at your elbow."

You obey.

"OK," you say. "No advice. But . . . I don't know, is there something that I ought to know and don't? Something you can tell me about Susan, or about Susan and me, that would help?"

"All I can say is that if everything goes belly-up and pear-shaped, you'll probably get over it and she probably won't."

You are shocked.

"That's not a very kind thing to say."

"I don't do kind, Paul. Truth isn't kind. You'll find that out soon enough as life kicks in."

"It feels as if it's kicked in pretty hard already."

"That may be all to the fucking good." Your face must look as if it's just taken a slap. "Come on, Paul, you didn't come all the way down here so that I'd give you a hug and tell you there are fairies at the bottom of the garden."

"True. Just tell me your thoughts on this.

165

Susan goes back to see Macleod every so often. Probably more than she says."

"Does that trouble you?"

"Mainly in the sense that if he ever lays a finger on her again, I'm going to have to kill him."

She laughs. "Oh, I do so miss the melodrama of being young."

"Don't patronise me, Joan."

"I'm not patronising you, Paul. Of course you'd do no such thing. But I admire you for the thought."

You wonder if she is being satirical. But Joan doesn't do satire.

"Why don't you think I would?"

"Because the last murder in the Village was probably committed by someone wearing woad."

You laugh, and take another sip of gin. "I'm worried," you say. "I'm worried that I shan't be able to save her."

She doesn't reply, and this annoys you.

"So what do you think about *that?*" you demand.

"I told you I'm not a fucking oracle. You might as well read your horoscope in the *Advertiser & Gazette.* I said when you ran away together, you've got guts, the pair of you. You've got guts, and you've got love. If that isn't good enough for life, then life isn't good enough for you."

"Now you are sounding like an oracle!"

"Then I'd better go and wash my mouth out with soap."

• • •

One day, you return to find her with cuts and bruises to her face, and her arms held defensively against her.

"I fell over that step in the garden," she says, as if it were a known hazard you had previously discussed. "I'm getting very trippy, I'm afraid."

She is indeed getting "trippy." Nowadays, as a reflex, you take her arm as you walk with her and keep watch for uneven pavements. But she also has a giveaway flush to her face. You call the doctor—not the private one she went to for her cheering-up pills.

Dr. Kenny is a fussy, inquisitive middle-aged man, but the right sort of GP—one who believes that house calls provide useful background when it comes to diagnosis. You take him upstairs to Susan's bedroom; her bruises are coming into full colour.

Downstairs again, he asks for a few words.

"Of course."

"It's rather puzzling," he begins. "It's unusual for a woman of her age to take a fall."

"She's been getting very trippy lately."

"Yes, that's the word she used to me. And, if I may ask, you are . . . ?"

"I'm her lodger . . . no, more than that, kind of godson, I suppose."

"Hmm. And it's just the two of you here?"

"There are two more lodgers in the attic

rooms." You decide not to promote Eric to the status of second godson.

"Does she have family?"

"Yes, but she's kind of . . . estranged from them at the moment."

"So she has no support? Except for you, that is?"

"I suppose not."

"As I say, it's rather puzzling. Do you think there was drink involved?"

"Oh no," you say swiftly, "she doesn't drink. She hates the stuff. That's one of the reasons she left her husband. He's a drinker. Flagons and gallons," you add, without being able to stop yourself.

You realise two things. First, that you lie automatically to protect Susan—even if the truth might have helped her more. You also begin to see how your relationship, or rather, your cohabitation, might appear to an outsider.

"So, if I may ask, what does she do all day?"

"She . . . does some volunteer work for the Samaritans." This isn't true either. Susan has mentioned the idea; though you are against it. You think she shouldn't try to start helping others when she is the one needing help.

"That's not much, is it?"

"Well, I suppose she . . . keeps house."

He looks around. The place is clearly in a mess. You realise that he is finding your answers inadequate. And why shouldn't he?

"If it happens again, we'll be obliged to investigate," he says. Then picks up his bag and leaves.

Investigate? you think. Investigate? He can tell you've been lying. But investigate what? Perhaps he guesses you are her lover, and suspects you might have been beating her up. Christ to that, you think: in your desire to protect her from being thought a drinker, you seem to be opening yourself up to a charge of assault. Perhaps he was giving you a final warning.

Not that the police would necessarily be interested. You remember an incident from a year or two before. You are in the car with Susan and have scarcely gone a quarter of a mile when you notice a couple rowing on the pavement. As you see the man bearing down on the woman you have flashbacks to the Macleod household. He is not exactly hitting her, but looks about to do so. Maybe they are drunk, you can't tell. You wind down the window and the woman yells, "Call the police!" Now he is holding her. "Call the police!" You speed home, dial 999, and are picked up by a patrol car which takes you to the scene of the reported possible crime. The couple have moved on, but you soon track them down a couple of streets away. They are ten yards apart, bellowing obscenities at one another.

"Oh, we know them," says the young constable. "It's just a domestic."

"Aren't you going to arrest him?"

The two of you are probably about the same age, but he knows he has seen more of life than you have.

"Well, sir, it's not our policy to interfere in domestics. I mean, not unless it really kicks off. They're just having a bit of a barney by the looks of it. Friday night, after all."

And then he drives the two of you home.

You realise that you want official interference into other people's lives but not into your own. You also realise that your truthfulness has become dangerously flexible. And you wonder if you should have got out of the car and tried to pull the man away from the woman.

One of your problems is this: for a long time it remains inconceivable to you that she is a drinker. How could she be, given that her husband is a drinker, and drink disgusts her? She hates even the smell of it, as she hates the bogus emotions it sets off in people. It makes Macleod coarser, angrier, more crudely sentimental; when he grabbed her hair and forced a glass to her lips, she would rather the sherry went down her dress than her throat. Nor has anyone in her life ever offered a credible counterexample: alcohol as glamorous, as usefully disinhibiting, as fun, as something you can control, knowing when to give the stuff its hour and when to refuse it.

You believe her. You never query her increasing lapses and latenesses. When you come in to find her blank-faced and bleary, you tell yourself that she has mistakenly swallowed an extra cheering-up pill—which is sometimes the case. And because you inevitably believe that one of the reasons she is on antidepressants is because you are failing to make her so happy that she doesn't need them, you feel guilty, and this guilt forbids you from questioning her. So when, out of her bleariness, she looks up, pats the sofa beside her, and asks,

"Where've you been all my life?"

you feel a ripping and a tearing inside you, and there is nothing you want more in the world than to make everything all right for her, and on her own terms, not yours. So you sit down next to her and take her wrists.

Just as you believe your love to be unique, you believe your problems—her problems—to be unique. You are too young to understand that all human behaviour falls into patterns and categories and that her—your—case is far from unique. You want her to be some kind of exception, rather than any kind of rule. If anyone had ventured such a word as codependency to you back then—assuming the term had even been invented—you would have laughed it off as American jargon. However, you might have been more impressed by a statistical linkage of which you were then unaware: that the partners of alcoholics, far from being repulsed by the habit—or rather, despite being repulsed by the habit—frequently succumb to it themselves.

But the next stage for you is to accept a percentage of the evidence in front of your eyes. You understand that in certain, very limited circumstances, she needs the small lift of a small drink—as she now occasionally admits. Obviously, she has to keep Joan company when she goes to the Village; obviously, she's sometimes frightened by the increasing traffic on the roads, and by that sudden twisty climb over the hills, so a little nip helps her; obviously, she is sometimes very lonely when you're away at college for most of the day. She also has "my bad time," as she calls it—usually between five and six in the evening, though as the days draw in and dusk falls earlier, so her bad time accordingly starts earlier, and obviously, extends just as late as it did before.

You believe what she says. You believe that the bottle she keeps beneath the sink, behind the bleach and washing-up liquid and silver polish, is the only bottle she drinks from. When she suggests that you put a pencil mark on the bottle so you can both monitor how much she drinks, you are heartened, and think these pencil marks are quite different from the ones on Eric's whisky bottle. Nor do you imagine there are other bottles elsewhere. When friends try to tip you off—"I'm a bit worried about Susan's drinking," says one, and "Boy, you could smell the booze from the other end of the phone," says another—you react in various ways. You protect her by denying it; you admit there are occasional lapses; you say the two of you have talked about it and she has promised "to see someone." You may even say all three things in the course of a single conversation. But you will also be offended by your friends' attempted helpfulness. Because you do not need help: the two of you, since you love one another, will be able to sort the matter out, thank you very much. And this slightly alienates your friends, and also alienates them from her. Increasingly, you find yourself saying, "She was just having a bad day," and you believe it yourself by dint of repetition.

Because there are still many good hours, and good days, when sobriety and cheerfulness fill the house, and her eyes and smile are just as they were when you first met, and you do something simple like drive for a walk in the woods, or go to the cinema and hold hands, and a sudden rush of feeling tells you it is all very easy and straightforward, and then your love is reaffirmed, yours for her, hers for you. And you wish you could display her to your friends at times like this: look, she is still herself, not just "underneath," but here, now, on the surface too.

173

You never suspect that one reason your friends tend to see her half-cut might be because she has persuaded herself, by some tortuous argument, that she needs a little Dutch courage before facing them.

Each stage rolls seamlessly into the next. And here comes a paradoxical one that you initially struggle with. If you love her, as you unwaveringly do, and if loving her means understanding her, then understanding her must include understanding why she is a drinker. You run through all her prehistory, and recent history, and current situation, and possible future. You understand all this, and before you know where you are, you have passed somehow from total denial of the fact that she drinks to total comprehension of why she might do so.

But with this comes a brute chronological fact. As far as you know, Susan only drank occasionally in all her years with Macleod. But now that she is living with you, she is—has become, is still becoming—an alcoholic. There is too much in this for you to entirely acknowledge, let alone bear.

She is sitting up in her quilted bedjacket, the newspapers around her, at her elbow a mug of coffee long gone cold. She has a frown on her, and her chin is pushed forward, as if she has been ruminating all day. It is now six in the evening, and you are in your last year of law studies. You sit on the side of her bed.

"Casey Paul," she begins, in an affectionate, puzzled tone, "I've decided that there's something seriously wrong."

"I think you may be right," you answer quietly. At last, you think, perhaps this is the moment of breakthrough. That's what's meant to happen, isn't it? Everything comes to a moment of crisis, and then the fever breaks, and all becomes clear and rational and happy again.

"But I've been searching my wits all day and can't get a handle on it."

Now where do you go? Do you start straight in again with the drinking? Suggest seeing the doctor again, a specialist, a psychiatrist? You are twenty-five, and quite untrained for this kind of situation. There are no articles in the newspaper headed, HOW TO COPE WITH YOUR MIDDLE-AGED FEMALE ALCOHOLIC LOVER. You are on your own. You have no theories of life yet, you only know some of its pleasures and pains. You still believe, however, in love, and in what love can do, how it can transform a life, indeed the lives of two people. You believe in its invulnerability, its tenacity, its ability to outrun any opponent. This, in fact, is your only theory of life so far.

So you do the best you can. You take one of her wrists, and talk about how you met and fell in love, how you were chosen by lot and then threw in your lot together, how you had run away in the finest tradition of lovers, and you continue like this, meaning and believing every word, and then you gently suggest that she's been drinking a little too much lately.

"Oh, you're always going on about that," she replies, as if this were some tedious and pedantic obsession of yours, nothing really to do with her. "But if you want me to say so, then I will. Maybe I occasionally take a drop or two more than is good for me."

You quell the prompting inner voice which says: No, not a drop or two, a whole bottle or two more than is good for you.

She goes on, "I'm talking about something much bigger than *that*. I think there's something seriously wrong."

"You mean, something that causes your drinking? Something I don't know about?" Your mind heads towards some terrible, defining event in her childhood, much worse than a "party kiss" from Uncle Humph.

"Oh, you really can be a Great Bore at times," she says mockingly. "No, much more important than that. What's behind it all."

You are already losing a little patience. "And what do you think might be behind it all?"

"Maybe it's the Russkis."

"The *Russkis?*" You—well, yes—you yelp.

"Oh Paul, do try and keep up. I don't mean the *actual* Russkis. They're just a figure of speech."

Like, say, the Ku Klux Klan or the KGB or the CIA or Che Guevara. You suspect that this one brief chance is slipping away, and you don't know if it is your fault, her fault, or nobody's fault.

"OK," you say. "The Russians are a figure of speech."

But she takes this only as sly impertinence.

"It's no good if you can't follow. There's something behind it all, just out of sight. Something which holds it all together. Something that, if we put it back together, would mend it all, would mend us all, don't you see?"

You give it your best shot. "You mean, like Buddhism?"

"Oh don't be absurd. You know what I think about religion."

"Well, it was just an idea," you say jokingly.

"And not a very good one."

How quickly it has gone from something tentative and gentle and hopeful to something irascible and mocking. And how far away from what you consider to be the problem, not just behind it all but on the surface and at all points in between: the bottles under the sink, under the bed, behind the bookshelves, in her stomach, in her head, in her heart. It may be true that you don't know the cause, if indeed there is a single, identifiable cause, but it seems to you that you can only work with—against—the manifestations that erupt every day.

You know what she means about religion, of course. There is her adamantine disapproval of missionaries, whether they seek to convert in distant lands or on suburban doorsteps. And there is also the Malta story, which she has told you more than once. When the girls were small, Gordon Macleod was posted to Malta for a couple of years. She went out and lived there for some of the time. And her abiding memory was of the priest's bicycle. Yes, she would explain, it's terribly Catholic out there. The church is all-powerful, and everyone's very obedient. And the church keeps them down by making the women have as many children as possible: it's absolutely impossible to obtain birth control on the island. They're very backward in that regard—John Bell & Croyden would be run out of town—so you have to take the equipment out with you.

Anyway, she goes on, it sometimes happens that a young bride doesn't get pregnant immediately after marriage, say for a year or two, despite all her prayers. Or maybe there's a woman who has two children and desperately wants a third but it isn't happening. And in such cases, the priest will come round and prop his bicycle outside the front door, so everyone—especially the husband—knows not to interfere until the bicycle has gone.

And when, nine months later—though of course it may take several goes—the family is blessed, that blessing is known as "the priest's child," and thought of as a gift from God. And sometimes there is more than one priest's child in the family. Can you imagine that, Paul? Don't you think it's barbaric?

You do think it's barbaric—you say so every time. And now part of you—the doomful, despairing, sarcastic part of you—wonders whether, if it isn't the Russkis who are behind it all, then it might be the Vatican.

You still share a bed, but haven't made love for a long time now. You don't ask yourself how long in calendar terms, because what counts is how it feels in terms of the heart. You discover more about sex than you want to—or more than you should be allowed to discover while still young. Certain discoveries should be kept for later in life, when they might hurt less.

You know already that there is good sex and bad sex. Naturally, you prefer good sex to bad sex. But also, being young, you think that even so, all things considered, taking the rough with the smooth, bad sex is better than no sex at all. And sometimes better than masturbation; though sometimes not.

But if you think these are the only categories of sex that exist, you find you are mistaken. Because there is a category which you had not known to exist, something which isn't, as you might have guessed had you heard about it before, merely a subcategory of bad sex; and that is sad sex. Sad sex is the saddest sex of all.

Sad sex is when, the toothpaste in her mouth not fully disguising the smell of sweet sherry, she whispers, "Cheer me up, Casey Paul." And you oblige. Though cheering her up also involves cheering yourself down.

Sad sex is when she is already doped by a cheering-up pill, but you think that if you fuck her, it might cheer her up a bit more.

Sad sex is when you are yourself in such despair, the situation so insoluble, the prehistory so oppressive, the very balance of your soul in doubt from day to day, moment to moment, that you think you may as well forget yourself for a few minutes, for half an hour, in sex. But you don't forget yourself, or your state of soul, not for even a nanosecond.

Sad sex is when you feel you are losing all touch with her, and she with you, but this is a way of telling one another that the connection is still there, somehow; that neither of you is giving up on the other, even if part of you fears that you should. Then you discover that insisting on the connection is the same as prolonging the pain.

Sad sex is when you are making love to a woman while thinking about how to kill her husband, even if this is something you would never be able to do, because you are not that sort of person. But as your body continues, so does your mind: you find yourself thinking, Yes, if you discovered him in the process of strangling her, you can imagine hitting him on the back of the head with a spade, or maybe stabbing him with a kitchen knife, though you realise that, given your hopelessness at fisticuffs, you might end up with the spade or the knife skidding off him and striking her instead. Then this parallel narrative in your head gets even madder, proposing that if you were to miss him and hit her instead, then it might be that you secretly wanted to harm her, because she—this woman now naked beneath you—has got you into this insoluble morass so early in your life.

Sad sex is when she is sober, you both desire one another, you know that you will always love her regardless, just as she will always love you regardless, but you—both of you, perhaps—now realise that loving one another does not necessarily lead to happiness. And so your lovemaking has become less a search for consolation than a hopeless attempt to deny your mutual unhappiness.

Good sex is better than bad sex. Bad sex is better than no sex, except when no sex is better than bad sex. Self-sex is better than no sex, except when no sex is better than self-sex. Sad sex is always far worse than good sex, bad sex, self-sex and no sex. Sad sex is the saddest sex of all.

At college you meet Paula—blond, friendly, direct—who has switched to law after a short-service commission in the Army. You like her handwriting when she shows you a case summary from a lecture you missed. You invite her for coffee one morning, then start having sandwich lunches in the nearby public gardens. One evening you take her to the cinema and kiss her good night. You exchange phone numbers.

A few days later, she asks, "Who's that mad-woman who lives in your house?"

"I'm sorry?" Already there is a chill spreading through you.

"I rang you up last night. A woman answered the phone."

"That would have been my landlady."

"She sounded as mad as a hatter."

You take a breath. "She's a little eccentric," you say. You want this conversation to stop, immediately. You wish it had never started. You wish Paula had never phoned the number you gave her. You very much don't want her to be specific, but you know she is going to be.

"I asked when you'd be back, and she said, 'Oh, he's very much the dirty stop-out, that young man, you can't rely on him from one moment to the next.' And then she came over all genteel and said something like, 'If you will excuse me while I fetch a pencil, I shall pass on any message you may choose to leave.' Well, I put the phone down before she came back."

She is looking at you expectantly, sure that you will provide her with an explanation that will satisfy her. It doesn't have to be much; a joke might even do it. Various extravagant lies cross your mind until, preferring the quarter-truth to the self-interested obfuscation—and also feeling stubborn and defensive about Susan—you repeat,

"She's a little eccentric."

And that, unsurprisingly, is the end of your relationship with Paula. And you realise that such a pattern is likely to repeat itself with other friendly and direct girls whose handwriting you admire.

Around this time, you stop thinking of her family by their nicknames. All that Mr. Elephant Pants and Miss Grumpy stuff was fine and funny at the time, part of the first silliness and proprietoriness of love. But it was also a facetious minimising of their presence in her life. And if you are beginning to think of yourself as grown-up— however forcedly and prematurely—then they should be allowed their own maturity as well.

Another thing you notice is that you no longer fall easily into the private, teasing love language that used to pass between you. Perhaps the weight of what you have taken on has temporarily crushed out love's decorativeness. Of course, you still love her, and tell her so, but in plainer terms nowadays. Perhaps, when you have solved her, or she has solved herself, there will be room again for such playfulness. You can't be sure.

Susan, however, continues using all the little phrases from her side of the relationship. It is her way of maintaining that nothing has changed, that she is fine, you are fine, all is fine. But she, you and it aren't, and those familiar words sometimes cause a prickle of embarrassment, more often lurching pain. You let yourself into the house, deliberately making enough noise to alert her, and as you come down the short flight of stairs into the kitchen, you find her in a familiar pose: red-faced by the gas fire, wrinkling her brow at a newspaper as if the world really does need to sort itself out. Then she looks up brightly and says, "Where've you been all my life?" or "Here's the dirty stop-out," and your cheerfulness—even if briefly assumed—drains like bathwater. You look around and take stock of the situation. You open the store cupboards to see if there is something you can make into something. And she lets you get on with it, while offering occasional remarks designed to convey that she is still well capable of understanding a newspaper.

"Things seem to be in a frightful mess, don't you agree, Casey Paul?"

And you ask, "Where exactly are we talking about?"

And she replies, "Oh, just about everywhere."

At which point you might throw the emptied tin of plum tomatoes into the bin with some force, and she will chide you,

"Temper, temper, Casey Paul!"

By months of manoeuvring, you get her first to a GP and then to a consultant psychiatrist at the local hospital. She doesn't want you to come with her, but you insist, knowing what will probably happen otherwise. You turn up at a quarter to three for a three o'clock slot. The waiting area already contains a dozen other patients, and you realise it is the hospital's policy to book everyone in for the same time, which is when the consultant's session begins. You can see their point: mad people—and at your age you use the term pretty broadly—are presumably not among the world's most punctilious timekeepers: so it's best to summon them all *en bloc*.

She makes what might be an attempt to escape, heading off to the ladies. You let her go with a fifty-fifty expectation that she won't return. But she does, and you find yourself reflecting cynically that she probably went to the hospital shop to check if they stocked booze, or maybe asked a few nurses where the bar was, only to receive the annoying news that the hospital doesn't have one.

You realise how sympathy and antagonism can coexist. You are discovering how many seemingly incompatible emotions can thrive, side by side, in the same human heart. You are angry with the books you have read, none of which have prepared you for this. No doubt you were reading the wrong books. Or reading them in the wrong way.

You feel, even at this late, desperate stage, that your emotional situation is still more interesting than that of your friends. They (mostly) have girlfriends and (mostly) have peer sex; some have been inspected by their girlfriends' parents, receiving approval, disapproval or judgement suspended. Most have a plan for their future life which includes this girlfriend—or, if not, one very similar. A plan to become furrow-dwellers. But for the moment, they have only the traditional clear-skinned joys, sane dreams and inchoate frustrations of young men in their mid-twenties with girlfriends of the same age. Yet here you are, in a hospital waiting area, surrounded by mad people, in love with a woman who is being characterised as potentially mad.

And the strange thing is, part of you feels exhilarated by it. You think: not only do you love Susan more than they love their girlfriends—

you must do, otherwise you wouldn't be sitting here among all the nutters—but you are having a more interesting life. They may measure their girlfriends' brains and breasts, and their future parent-in-laws' deposit accounts, and imagine they have won; but you are still ahead of them because your relationship is more fascinating, more complicated and more insoluble. And the proof of this is that you are sitting here on a metal stacking chair, half-reading some discarded magazine, while your beloved dreams of—what? Escape, no doubt: escape from here, escape from you, escape from life? She too is staggering beneath the weight of extreme, unbearable and incompatible emotions. You are both in deep pain. And yet, aware as you are of the stupid, bolloxy world of male competitiveness, you tell yourself that you are still a winner. And when you get to this point in your thoughts, the next logical stage is: you're a nutter as well. You are obviously one stark staring, complete and utter nutter. On the other hand, you are the youngest fucking nutter in the whole waiting area. So you have won again! Former under-12, under-6-stone school boxing champion becomes hospital's under-26 nutter champion!

At this moment a round, bald, suited man opens the door of the consulting room.

"Mr. Ellis," he calls quietly.

There is no reply. Familiar with the inattention,

selective deafness and other failings of his patients, the consultant raises his voice:

"Mr. ELLIS!"

Some old fool wearing three sweaters and an anorak gets to his feet; a towelling headband restrains the ten or so wisps of white hair that sprawl from his crown. He stands looking round for a moment, as if perhaps expecting applause for having recognised his own name, then follows the consultant into his office.

You are not prepared for what happens next. You hear the psychiatrist's voice, quite clearly, say,

"And how are we today, Mr. Ellis?"

You look at the closed door. You see that there is a three-inch gap between the foot of it and the floor. You guess that the consultant must be facing the door. You do not hear a reply from the deaf old fool, but perhaps there hasn't been one, because next, loud enough to rouse the other nodding nutters, come the words,

"SO HOW'S THE DEPRESSION, MR. ELLIS?"

You are not sure if Susan has been paying attention. For yourself, you think this is unlikely to work.

There is her shame, which is ever present. And then there is your shame, which sometimes presents itself as pride, sometimes as a kind of noble realism; but also, mostly, as what it is—just shame.

You come back one evening to find her pie-eyed in a chair, the water glass by her side still containing a good inch or so of non-water. You decide to behave as if all this is completely normal—indeed, what domestic life is all about. You go into the kitchen and start looking around for something to turn into something. You find some eggs: you ask if she would like an omelette.

"It's easy for you," she answers belligerently.

"What's easy for me?"

"That's a clever lawyer's answer," she replies, taking a swig right in front of you, which she rarely does. You are about to go back to cracking eggs, when she adds,

"Gerald died today."

"Which Gerald?" You can't immediately think of a Gerald among your mutual friends.

"Which Gerald indeed? Mr. Clever. *My* Gerald. My Gerald that I told you about. The one I was engaged to. This was the day he died."

You feel terrible. Not because you have forgotten the date—she has never told you it before—but because, unlike you, she has her dead to remember. Her fiancé, the brother who disappeared out over the Atlantic, Gordon's father—whose name you no longer remember—who had been soft on her. You have no such figures in your life, no griefs, no holes, no losses. So you don't know what it's like. Everyone should remember their dead, you believe, and everyone else should respect this need and desire. You are in fact rather envious, and wish you had a few dead of your own.

Later, you become more suspicious. She has never mentioned the day of Gerald's death before. And there is no way for you to check. Just as, in happier days, there was no way for you to check when she told you how many times the two of you had made love. Perhaps, when she heard your key turn in the lock, and she was unable to get up and also unwilling to hide the glass at her elbow, she decided—no, this is perhaps too deliberate a verb to describe her mental processes that evening—she "realised," yes, she suddenly realised that it was the day of Gerald's death. Though it could equally have been Alec's, or that of Gordon's father. Who could tell? Who knew? And who, in the end, cared?

I said I never kept a diary. This isn't strictly true. There was a point, in my isolation and turmoil, when I thought writing things down might help. I used a hardback notebook, black ink, one side of the paper. I tried to be objective. There was no point, I thought, in merely venting my feelings of hurt and betrayal. I remember that the first line I wrote down was:

All alcoholics are liars.

This was, obviously, not based on a huge sample or broad research. But I believed it at the time, and now, decades later, with more field experience, I believe it to be an essential truth about the condition. I went on:

All lovers are truth-tellers.

Again, the sample was small, consisting mainly of myself. It seemed to me evident that love and truth were connected; indeed, as I may have said, that to live in love is to live in truth.

And then the conclusion to this quasi-syllogism:

Therefore, the alcoholic is the opposite of the lover.

This seemed not just logical, but also consistent with my observations.

Nowadays, a lifetime later, the second of these propositions seems the weakest. I have seen too many examples of lovers who, far from living in truth, dwelt in some fantasy land where self-delusion and self-aggrandizement reigned, with reality nowhere to be found.

Yet, even while I was compiling my notebook, searching to be objective, the subjective kept undermining me. For instance, I realised, looking back at our time in the Village, that whereas I thought of myself as both lover and truth-teller, the truths I had told were only to myself and Susan. I told lies to my parents, to Susan's family, to my own close friends; I even dissembled at the tennis club. I protected the zone of truth with a rampart of lies. Just as she was now lying to me all the time about her drinking. As well as lying to herself. And yet she would still affirm that she loved me.

So I began to suspect that I was wrong in considering alcoholism as the opposite of love. Perhaps they were much closer than I imagined. Alcoholism is certainly just as obsessive—as absolutist—as love; and maybe to the drinker the hit of booze is as powerful as the hit of sex is to the lover. So could the alcoholic be merely a lover who has shifted the object and focus of his or her—no, her—love?

My observations and reflections had filled a few dozen pages when I came home one evening to find Susan in a state I knew all too well: red-faced, semi-coherent, quick to take offence, yet at the same time genteelly pretending that all was for the best in this best possible of worlds. I went to my room and discovered that my desk had been inexpertly rifled. I had, even then, a habit of orderliness, and knew what lived where. Since the desk contained my Notes on Alcoholism, I assumed, wearily, that she had probably read them. Still, I thought, perhaps in the long run the shock might have a useful effect on her. In the short run, evidently not.

The next time I went to my notebook to make an addition, I saw that Susan had done more than just read it. She had left an annotation beneath my last entry, using the same black ink from the same pen. In an unsteady hand, she had written:

With your inky pen to make you hate me.

I didn't accuse her of rifling my desk, reading my notebook, writing in it. I could imagine her saying, in a tone of polite protest, "No, I don't think so." I was weary of constant confrontation. But then, I was equally weary of a constant pretence that all was well, a constant evasion of the truth. I also realised that it would be impossible for me to write anything down in the future without picturing her at my desk studying my latest denunciations. This would be intolerable for both of us: the annotation of pain on my part, the dim yet irate acknowledgement of pain caused on her part. So I threw away the notebook.

But that half-formed sentence of hers, written by a wonky hand with an unfamiliar pen, remained with me, and always has. Not least because of its ambiguity. Did she mean, "You use your inky pen to write down things which will then make you hate me"? Or did she mean, "I have left my mark with your inky pen because I want to make you hate me"? Critical and aggressive, or masochistic and self-pitying? Maybe she knew what she meant when she wrote the words, but there was no subsequent clarity to be found. You may judge the second interpretation oversubtle, and designed to let me off the hook. But—and this formed the basis of another of my long-lost notes—the alcoholic, in my experience, wants to provoke, to push away help, to justify her own isolation. So if she managed to convince herself that I hated her, all the more reason to turn for comfort to the bottle.

You are taking her somewhere in the car. There is no need for her to fear the journey, and you will pick her up later and drive her home. But there are the usual delays before you can get her into the car. And as you are about to release the handbrake, she rushes back into the house and returns with a large, bright yellow plastic laundry bag, which she puts between her feet. She does not explain. You do not ask. This is where things have got to.

And then you think, Oh Fuckit.

"What's that for?" you ask.

"The thing is," she replies, "I'm not feeling entirely well, and it's just possible I might be sick. What with the car and all that."

No, you think, what with being drunk and all that. A doctor friend has told you that alcoholics sometimes throw up so violently that they can perforate their own oesophagus. As it happens, she doesn't need to vomit, but she might as well have done. Because she has already filled your head with an image of her throwing up into this yellow bag, and you cannot stop seeing it. You might as well have listened to her dry retching and then wet retching, and can hear the vomit trickling into the bright yellow plastic. The smell, too, of course, in your small car. The excuses, the lies. Her lies, your lies.

Because it is no longer just a question of her lying to you. When she does so, you have two choices: call her out on it, or accept what she says. Usually, out of weariness and a desire for peace—and yes, out of love—you accept what she says. You condone the lie. And so become a liar by proxy. And it is a very short step from accepting her lies to lying yourself—out of weariness, and a desire for peace, and also out of love—yes, that too.

What a long way you have come. Years ago, when you started off lying to your parents, you did so with a kind of relish, reckless of consequence; it almost felt character-building. Later, you began to tell lies in all directions: to protect her, and to protect your love. Later still, she starts lying to you, to keep you from knowing her secret; and now she lies with a kind of relish, reckless of consequence. Then, finally, you begin lying to her. Why? Something to do with the need to create some internal space which you could keep intact—and where you could yourself remain intact. And this is how it is for you now. Love and truth—where have they gone?

You ask yourself: Is staying with her an act of courage on your part, or an act of cowardice? Perhaps both? Or is it just an inevitability?

She has taken to going to the Village by train. You approve: you think this comes from a recognition of her unfitness to drive. You take her to the station, she tells you the time of her return train, though, as often as not, she doesn't turn up until the next one, or the one after. And when she says, "Don't bother meeting me," she is protecting her inner world. And when you reply, "Fine—sure you'll be all right?" you are protecting yours.

The phone goes one evening.

"Is that Henry?"

"No, sorry, wrong number."

You are about to put the phone down when the man reads your number to you.

"Yes, that's right."

"Well, good evening, sir. This is the transport police at Waterloo Station. We have a lady here in a . . . slightly distressed condition. We found her asleep in the train and, well, her handbag was open and there was a sum of money in it, so you see . . ."

"Yes I see."

"She showed us this number and asked us to call Henry."

In the background you hear her voice. "Call Henry, call Henry."

Ah, her shorthand for Henry Road.

So you drive to Waterloo, find the office of the railway police and there she is, sitting up, bright-eyed, waiting to be collected, knowing that it would happen. The two policemen are courteous and concerned. They are doubtless used to helping drunk old ladies found snoring in empty carriages. Not that she is old, just that when she is drunk, you think of her, suddenly, as a drunk old lady.

"Well, thank you very much for looking after her."

"Oh, she was no trouble at all, sir. Quiet as a mouse. Look after yourself, Madam."

She gives a rather stately acknowledging nod. You take the arm of this piece of left luggage, and off you go. Your annoyance and despair, however, are cut by a certain pride in her having been "no trouble." Though what if she had been?

Eventually, more out of despair than hope, you try tough love, or at least what your understanding of that concept is. You don't let her get away with anything. You call her out on her lies. You pour away whatever bottles you find, some in obvious places, some in such strange locations that she must have hidden them there while drunk, and then forgotten where she had put them. You get her banned from the three local shops which sell alcohol. You give them each a photo to keep behind the till. You do not tell her this; you think the humiliation of being refused service will jolt her. You never find out, and she merely gets round the obstruction by travelling further afield.

You hear reports. Some people are shy about mentioning things to you, others not. A friend, on a bus a mile or so away from Henry Road, has spotted her down an alleyway next to an off-licence, raising a newly bought bottle to her lips. This image burns deep, and transforms itself from another's account into your own private memory. A neighbour tells you that your auntie was in the Cap and Bells last Saturday night, downing five sherries in succession until they stopped serving her. "It's not the kind of pub someone like her should be in," the neighbour adds concernedly. "They get all sorts in there." You picture the scene, from her ashamed first order at the bar to her unsteady walk home, and this too becomes part of your memory bank.

You tell her that her behaviour is destroying your love for her. You do not mention hers for you.

"Then you must leave me," she says. She is flushed, dignified and logical.

You know that you are not going to do this. The question is, whether or not she knows it too.

You write her a letter. If spoken words of rebuke fly unhindered straight out of her head, perhaps written ones will stick. You tell her that the way she is going on, she will almost certainly die of a wet brain, that there is nothing more you can do for her, except come to her funeral, whenever that might be. You leave the letter on the kitchen table, in an envelope with her name on it. She never mentions receiving it, opening it, reading it. *With your inky pen to make you hate me.*

You realise that tough love is also tough on the lover.

You are taking her to Gatwick. Martha has invited her out to Brussels, where she is working as a Eurocrat. To your surprise, Susan agrees. You promise to make it as easy as possible for her. You will drive her to the airport and see her through check-in. She nods, then says straightforwardly,

"You might have to let me have a drink before getting on the plane. Belgian courage."

You are more than relieved: almost encouraged.

The night before she is half-packed and half-drunk. You go to bed. She continues packing and drinking. The next morning she comes to you with a cupped hand over her mouth.

"I'm afraid I don't think I shall be able to go."

You look at her without speaking.

"I've lost my teeth. I can't find them anywhere. I think I may have thrown them into the garden."

You don't say anything except, "We have to leave by two." You decide to let her go on destroying her life.

But perhaps your failure to respond—to offer neither help nor rebuke—is, for once, the correct approach. An hour or two later, she is walking around with her teeth in, never alluding to either having lost them, or found them.

At two o'clock you put her case in the back of the car, double-check her ticket and passport and set off. There have been no last-minute diversions, no scurrying for a bright yellow laundry bag. She sits beside you quiet as a mouse, in the railway policeman's words.

As you are approaching Redhill, she turns and says in a demurely puzzled way, as if you were more her chauffeur than her lover,

"Would you mind very much telling me where we are going?"

"You're going to Brussels. To visit Martha."

"Oh, I don't think so. There must be some mistake."

"That's why you've got your ticket and your passport in your handbag." Though they are actually in your pocket, as you don't want them going the way of her teeth.

"But I don't know where she lives."

"She's meeting you at the airport."

There is a pause.

"Yes," she says, nodding, "I seem to remember about this now."

There is no further resistance. Part of you thinks she should have a large label round her neck with her name and destination written on it, like a wartime refugee. With perhaps her gas mask in a box as well.

At the bar you buy her a double schooner of sherry, which she sips with inattentive gentility. You think: it could be worse. This is how you react to situations nowadays. You have the lowest of expectations.

The trip turns out to be a success. She has been shown the city, and brings you some postcards. Miss Grumpy, she announces, is nowadays Much Less So, perhaps influenced by a charming Belgian boyfriend who was in attendance. Her memories are clearer than usual, a sign that she has been temperate. You feel happy for her, if slightly resentful that she can clean up her act for others more easily than for you. Or so it seems.

But then, she tells you that on the last morning, the real reason why her daughter invited her out became clear. She, Miss Grumpy, is of the opinion that her mother ought to go back to

Mr. Gordon Macleod. Who is now very contrite and promises to be on his best behaviour if she returns. According to Susan, according to her daughter.

To save time, and to save emotion, you address her, straightforwardly, as a drinker. No longer, There seems to be a problem, Do you know what it might be, Perhaps I can suggest . . . none of that. So one day you suggest Alcoholics Anonymous, not knowing if there is a branch near you.

"Not going to the God-botherers," she replies firmly.

Given her dislike of priests, and extreme disapproval of missionaries, this response is understandable. No doubt she thinks of AA as yet another bunch of American missionaries interfering in other countries' belief systems, bringing the foreign halt and lame into the radiant presence of their God. You do not blame her.

Mostly, you can only deal with the day-to-day crises. Occasionally, you look to the future, and find one outcome which has a terrifying logic. It goes like this. She doesn't drink all the time. Not every day. She can go a day or two without the comfort of a bottle. But her memory, as a result of the drink, is getting poorer. So the logic runs: if she carries on destroying her memory at the present rate, maybe she will reach the stage when she has actually forgotten she is an alcoholic!

Might that happen? It would be one way to cure her. But you also think: you might as well simply blast her with ECT and be done with it.

Here is one of the problems. You don't, at bottom, think of alcoholism as a physical disease. You might have heard that it is, but you aren't really convinced. You can't help thinking of it as many people—some of whom you might not want to be associated with—have thought about it for centuries: as a moral disease. And one of the reasons you do so is because she does too. When she is at her most lucid, her most rational, her most gentle, and as much tormented by what is happening to her as you are, she tells you—as she always has—that she hates the fact that she is a drinker, and feels deep shame and guilt about it: so you must leave her, because she is "no good." She has a moral disease, which is why hospitals and doctors cannot cure her. They cannot fix a flawed personality from a played-out generation. She urges you again to leave her.

But you cannot leave Susan. How could you bear to withdraw your love from her? If you didn't love her, who would? And maybe it is worse than this. It is not just that you love her, but that you are addicted to her. How ironic would that be?

An image comes into your head one day, an image of your relationship to one another. You are at an upstairs window of the house on Henry Road. She has somehow climbed out, and you are hanging on to her. By the wrists, of course. And her weight makes it impossible for you to pull her back inside. It is all you can do to stop yourself being pulled out with her, by her. At one point she opens her mouth to scream, but no sound emerges. Instead, her dental plate comes loose; you hear it hit the ground with a plasticky clatter. You are stuck there, the two of you, locked together, and will remain so until your strength gives out, and she falls.

It is only a metaphor—or the worst of dreams; yet there are metaphors which sit more powerfully in the brain than remembered events.

Another image, based on a remembered event, comes into your mind. You are back at the Village, the two of you, in the flush of love, quietly but entirely intent on one another. She is wearing a print dress and, knowing that you are watching her—because you are always watching her—she goes over to the chintzy sofa, plumps herself down, and says,

"Look, Casey Paul, I'm disappearing! I'm doing my disappearing act!"

And, for a moment, as you look, you can see only her face and the stockinged part of her legs.

Now she is doing another disappearing act. Her body is still there, but what lies inside—

her mind, her memory, her heart—is slipping away. Her memory is obscured by darkness and untruth, and persuades itself towards coherence only by fabulation. Her mind oscillates between stunned inertia and hysterical volatility. But it is the disappearing act which her heart is doing, oh, that is the hardest part to bear. It is as if, in her thrashing about, she has stirred up the mud that lies at the bottom of us all. And what is now coming to the surface is unfocussed anger, and fear, and frustration, and harshness, and selfishness and mistrust. When she tells you solemnly that in her considered opinion your behaviour towards her has been not just beastly but actively criminal, she really thinks it is true. And all the sweetness of her nature, the laughingness and trustingness central to the woman you fell in love with, can no longer be seen.

You used to say—when putting off friends who wanted to visit—"Oh, she's having a bad day. She's not herself." And when they saw her drunk, you'd say, "But she's still the same underneath. She's still the same underneath." How many times did you tell this to others, when the person you were actually addressing was yourself?

And then comes the day when you no longer believe such words. You no longer believe that she is still the same underneath. You believe that being "not herself" is her new self. You fear that she is, finally and utterly, doing her disappearing act.

But you make one final effort, and she does too. You get her admitted to hospital. Not the National Temperance, as you had hoped, but a general, all-female ward. You sit her down on a bench while they are admitting her, and explain gently, once more, how it has come to this, and what they will do for her, and how it will help.

"I'll give it my very best shot, Casey Paul," she says sweetly. You kiss her on the temple, and promise to visit her every day. Which you do.

At first they put her to sleep for three days, hoping to peaceably flush the alcohol out of her system, while also calming her disturbed brain. You sit by her lightly sleeping form and think that this time, surely, it will work. This time, she is under proper medical supervision, the problem has been stated clearly—even she isn't ducking it—and at last Something Will Be Done. You look at her calm face and think of the best years of your time together, and imagine that everything you had back then will now return.

On the fourth day she is still asleep when you go in. You ask to see a doctor and some twenty-year-old houseman with a clipboard presents himself. You ask why she is still sedated.

"We woke her up this morning, but she immediately became disruptive."

"Disruptive?"

"Yes, she attacked the nurses."

You don't believe this. You ask him to repeat it. He does.

"So we put her under again. Don't worry, it's a very light sedative. I'll show you."

He adjusts the drip slightly. Almost instantly, she begins to stir. "You see?" Then he adjusts the drip again and sends her back to sleep. You find this deeply sinister. You have yielded her care to the authority of some youthful technocrat who has never met her.

"You're her . . . ?"

"Godson," you reply automatically. Or maybe you say "Nephew," or possibly "Lodger," which at least contains four correct letters in it.

"Well, if we wake her up and she's that disruptive again, we'll have to section her."

"*Section* her?" You are horrified. "But she's not mad. She's an alcoholic, she needs treatment."

"So do all the other patients. And they need the nurses' attention. We can't have nurses being attacked." You still don't believe his initial allegation.

"But . . . you can't just section her by yourself."

"You're right, there have to be two signatures. But it's just a formality in cases like this."

You realise you have not brought her to a place of safety after all. You have delivered her over to the kind of zealot who in the old days would have prescribed a straitjacket plus a course of electroconvulsive therapy. Susan would have called him a "little Hitler." Who knows, perhaps she did. You partly hope so.

You say, "I would like to be there when you next wake her up. I think it would help."

"Very well," says the curt young man whom you have already come to hate deeply.

But—such is the way of hospitals—this arrogant little shit isn't there when you next come, and you never see him again. Instead, a female doctor operates the drip. Slowly, Susan wakes. She looks up, sees you and smiles.

"Where've you been all my life?" she asks. "You dirty stop-out."

The doctor reacts with slight surprise, but you kiss Susan on the forehead, and the two of you are left alone together.

"So you've come to take me home?"

"Not just yet, darling," you say. "You've got to stay here for a while. Until you're cured."

"But there's nothing wrong with me. I'm perfectly well and insist on being taken home at once. Take me to Henry."

You grasp both her wrists. You squeeze very hard. You explain that the doctors won't release her until she is cured. You remind her of the promise she made when you brought her here. You say that the last time they brought her round, she attacked the nurses.

"No, I don't think so," she says, in her most distant, genteel manner, as if you are some ill-informed peasant.

You talk at length to her, asking for her promise to behave until you come back tomorrow. At least until then. She doesn't respond. You press her. Then she promises, but with a stubbornness of tone you are all too familiar with.

The next day, you approach the ward expecting the worst: that she's been sedated again, or even sectioned. But she is looking alert, and her colour is good. She greets you rather as if you were her guest. A nurse walks by.

"The maids here are frightfully good," she says, giving a wave to the passing figure.

You think: What's the right tactic? Go along with it? Challenge it? You decide that you mustn't indulge her dream world.

"They're not maids, Susan, they're nurses." You think she might have confused "hospital" with "hotel," which after all would not be much of a verbal slippage.

"Some of them are," she agrees. Then, disappointed with your lack of perspicacity, adds, "But most of them are maids."

You let it go.

"I've told them all about you," she says.

Your heart sinks, but you let that go as well.

The next day, you find her agitated again. She is out of bed, sitting up in a chair. On the tray in front of her are five pairs of spectacles and a copy of a P. G. Wodehouse novel she has mysteriously acquired.

"Where did you get all those glasses?"

"Oh," she replies casually, "I don't know where they come from. I expect people have been giving them to me."

She puts on a pair which are evidently not hers and opens the book at random. "He's frightfully funny, isn't he?"

You agree. She has always enjoyed Wodehouse, and you take this as a good, if slightly confused, sign. You tell her what's in the newspapers. You mention a postcard you've had from Eric. You say that all is well at Henry Road. She listens idly then seizes a different pair of glasses—though still not her own—opens the book at random again and, probably seeing it no more in focus than the previous time, announces,

"It's frightful rubbish, this, isn't it?"

You think your heart will break, now, here, immediately.

The following day she is again under sedation. The woman in the next bed chats to you and asks what's wrong with Your Nan. You are so weary of it all that you answer,

"She's an alcoholic."

The woman turns away in distaste. You know exactly what she is thinking. Why give a good hospital bed to a drinker? Furthermore, a female drinker? One thing you have discovered is that male alcoholics are allowed to be amusing, even poignant. Young drinkers of either sex, when out of control, are indulged. But female alcoholics, old enough to know better, old enough to be mothers, even grandmothers—these are the lowest of the low.

The next day she is awake again and refusing to look at you. So you just sit there for a while. You glance at the tray in front of her. This time, her nocturnal ward-rambling has netted only two pairs of other patients' glasses, plus a tabloid newspaper she would never have in the house.

"I do think," she announces finally, "that you will be remembered as one of the greatest criminals in the history of the world."

You are tempted to agree. Why not?

They do not threaten to section her—that little Hitler is off practising his black arts on other, less disruptive patients. But they tell you that they cannot treat her further, that the rest may have done her some good, that this is not the appropriate place for her and they need to free up the bed. You see their point of view entirely, but ask yourself: Then what is the appropriate place for her? Which stands in for a wider question: What is her place in the world?

As the two of you leave, the woman in the next bed pointedly ignores you both.

• • •

It has taken some years for you to realise how much, beneath her laughing irreverence, there lies panic and pandemonium. Which is why she needs you there, fixed and steadfast. You have assumed this role willingly, lovingly. It makes you feel grown-up to be a guarantor. It has meant, of course, that for most of your twenties you were obliged to forgo what others of your generation routinely enjoyed: the mad fucking around, the hippie travelling, the drugs, the going off the rails, even the stonking idleness. You were also obliged to forgo the drinking; but then, you were hardly living with a good advertisement for the stuff. You didn't hold any of this against her (except perhaps the lack of drinking); nor did you treat it as some unfair burden you were assuming. It was just the given of your relationship. And it has made you age, or mature, if not by the route normally taken.

But as things begin to fray between you, and all your attempts to rescue her fail, you acknowledge something you haven't exactly been hiding from, just didn't have time to notice: that the particular dynamic of your relationship is triggering your own version of panic and pandemonium. While you probably strike your friends at law college as affable and sane, if a little withheld, what roils beneath your own surface is a mixture of groundless optimism and searing anxiety.

Your inner moods ebb and flow in response to hers: except that her cheerfulness, even when misplaced, strikes you as authentic, your own as conditional. How long will this present little stretch of happiness last, you are continually asking yourself. A month, a week, another twenty minutes? You can't, of course, tell, because it doesn't depend on you. And however calming your presence is on her, the trick doesn't work the other way round.

You never think of her as a child, not even in her most selfish delinquencies. But when you watch an anxious parent tracking its offspring— the alarm at each bandy-legged footstep, the fear of each "trippy" moment, the wider fear of the child simply wandering off and getting lost—you know that you have been there yourself. Not to mention the child's sudden switches of mood, from blissful exaltation and absolute trust to rage and tears and a sense of abandonment. This too is familiar. Except that this wild, shifting weather of the soul is now passing through the brain and body of a mature woman.

It is this, finally, which breaks you, and tells you to move out. Not far, just a dozen streets, into a cheap one-room flat. She urges you to go, for reasons good and bad: because she senses that she must let you go a little if she is to keep you and because she wants you out of the house so that she can drink whenever the mood takes her. But in fact, little changes: you are still living just as closely. She doesn't want you to remove a single book from your study, or any knick-knack you have bought together, or any clothes from your wardrobe: such actions will throw her into a fit of grieving. Sometimes you sneak back into the house to remove a book, shuffling others along the shelf to cover the theft; occasionally, you stuff in a couple of cheap paperbacks from Oxfam to disguise the betrayal.

And so you live an oscillating life. You continue to have breakfast with her, and also supper—which you mostly cook; you go on expeditions together; and you get reports from Eric on her drinking. Eric, being merely fond and concerned, rather than in love with her, is a more reliable witness than you ever were yourself. Susan continues to do your laundry, and some of your best shirts come back lovingly scorched. Drunken ironing: that is one of the lesser, but still painful, things life has surprised you with.

Then, almost without your noticing it, what is close to the final stage kicks in. You may still desperately want to save her, but at some level of instinct or pride or self-protection, her devotion to drink now strikes you more sharply, and more personally: as a rejection of you, of your help, of your love. And since few can bear to have their love rejected, resentment builds, then curdles into aggression, and you find yourself saying—not aloud, of course, because you find it hard to be overtly cruel, especially to her—"Go on, then, destroy yourself, if that's what you want." And you are shocked to discover yourself thinking this.

But what you don't realise—not now, in the heat and dark of it all, only much later—is that, even without hearing you, she will agree. Because what she is leaving unspoken is this reply: "Yes, that's exactly what I want. And I *am* going to destroy myself, because I am a worthless person. So stop bothering me with your well-intentioned meddling. Just let me get on with the job."

You are working for a South London practice which specialises in legal aid. You enjoy the range of cases you handle; you enjoy the fact that in the majority of them you can solve things. You can get people the justice they deserve, and thereby make them happy. You are aware of the paradox of this. Also, of another, longer-term paradox: that in order to support Susan, you need to work, and the more you work, the more you are away from her, and the less able to support her.

You have also, as Susan predicted, found yourself a girlfriend. And not one who will run off at the first phone call. Anna is, perhaps inevitably, also a lawyer. You have told her some of Susan's history. You have not tried to get away with merely saying she is "eccentric." You introduce the two of them, and they seem to get on. Susan says nothing to embarrass you, Anna is brightly practical. She doesn't think Susan looks after her diet well enough, so once a week takes round a loaf of proper bread, a bag of tomatoes, a pound of French butter. Sometimes the door remains unanswered, so she leaves her offering on the step.

You are home one evening when the phone goes. It is one of the lodgers.

"I think you'd better come round. We've had the police. With guns."

You repeat the words to Anna, then run for your car. In Henry Road there is an ambulance outside the house, its blue light revolving, its doors open. You park, walk across, and there she is, in a wheelchair facing out towards the street, with a broad bandage around her forehead which has pushed her hair up into a *Struwwelpeter* shock. Her expression, as often when a sudden crisis has worked itself out, is one of slightly amused calm. She surveys the street, the ambulance men fixing the wheelchair in place, and your own arrival, as if from a throne. The blue light revolves against the steadier sodium orange. It is real and unreal at the same time; filmic, phantasmagoric.

Then the chair slowly rises on its hoist, and as the ambulance doors are about to be closed, she lifts her hand in a pontifical blessing. You ask the ambulance men where they are taking her and follow in your car. When you get to the A&E department, they are already taking preliminary details.

"I'm her next of kin," you say.

"Son?" they ask. You nearly agree, for speed, but they might query the difference of surname. So, once again, you are her nephew.

"He's not really my nephew," she says. "I could tell you a thing or two about this young man."

You look at the doctor, lying to him with a slight frown and a tiny movement of the head. You collude in the notion that Susan is temporarily off among the nutters.

"Ask him about the tennis club," she says.

"We'll come to that, Mrs. Macleod. But first . . ."

And so the process continues. They will keep her in overnight, perhaps run a test or two. It may just be shock. They will call you when they are ready to release her. The ambulance men have said it was just a cut, but as it was on the forehead there was a lot of blood. It may need a stitch or two, maybe not.

The next day, they release her, still in full dispossession of her faculties.

"About time too," she says, as you walk her to the car park. "It really has all been frightfully interesting."

You know this mood only too well. Something has been observed, or experienced, or discovered, which has little to do with anything, yet is of extreme, overwhelming interest, and must be reported.

"Let's wait until we get you home first." You have slipped into the language of the hospital, where everything is done or asked for in the name of "us."

"All right, Mr. Spoilsport."

At Henry Road, you take her to the kitchen, sit her down, make her a cup of tea with extra sugar and give her a biscuit. She ignores them.

"Well," she begins, "it was all so fascinating. Such fun. You see, these two men with guns got into the house last night."

"With *guns?*"

"That's what I said. With guns. Do stop interrupting before I've barely even started. So yes, two men with guns. And they were going round looking for something. I don't know what."

"Were they robbers?" You feel you are allowed to ask questions which don't challenge the essential veracity of her fantasy.

"Well, that's what I thought might be the case. So I said to them, 'The gold bullion is under the bed.'"

"Wasn't that a bit rash?"

"No, I thought it would put them off the scent. Not that I knew what the scent was, of course.

They were both quite polite and well mannered. For gunmen, that is. They didn't want to bother me, they would just go about their business if I didn't mind."

"But didn't they shoot at you?" You indicate her forehead, now decorated with a large gauze patch.

"Lord, no, they were much too polite for that. But it was rather an interruption to the evening, so I felt obliged to call the police."

"Didn't they try and stop you?"

"Oh no, they were all in favour. They agreed with me that the police might help them find what they were looking for."

"But they didn't tell you what that was?"

She ignores you and continues.

"But the thing I really wanted to tell you was that they had these feathers everywhere."

"Gosh."

"Feathers sticking out of their bottoms. Feathers in their hair. Feathers everywhere."

"What sort of guns did they have?"

"Oh, who knows about guns?" she says dismissively. "But then the police came, and I answered the door to them, and they sorted everything out."

"Was there a gunfight?"

"A gunfight? Don't be ridiculous. The British police are far too professional for that."

"But they arrested them?"

"Naturally. Why else do you think I called them?"

"So how did you cut your head?"

"Well, of course I can't remember that. It's the least interesting part of the story in my view."

"I'm glad it all worked out in the end."

"You know, Paul," she says, "sometimes I'm really disappointed in you. It was so enjoyable and so fascinating, but you keep coming up with these banal comments and banal questions. Of course it all worked out in the end. Everything always does, doesn't it?"

You don't answer. After all, you have your pride. And in your opinion, the notion that everything works out in the end, and the counternotion that nothing ever does, are both equally banal.

"Now don't sulk. It's been one of the most interesting twenty-four hours of my life. And everyone—*everyone*—was very nice to me indeed."

The gunmen. The police. The ambulance men. The hospital. The Russkis. The Vatican. And all's right with the world, then.

That evening, over takeaway pizzas, I recounted the whole lurid episode to Anna. I told it fondly, concernedly, almost amusedly, if not quite. The fantasy gunmen, the real policemen, the gold bullion, the feathers, the ambulance men, the hospital. I omitted some of Susan's strictures on my character. I was also aware, however, that Anna was not reacting as I had expected.

Eventually, she said, "That all sounds a great waste of public money."

"That's an odd way to look at it."

"Is it? Police, firearms squad—Special Branch—ambulance, hospital. All of them dashing around making a fuss of her, just because she's gone on a bender. And that includes you too."

"Me? What do you expect me to do when the lodger calls and says there are armed police in the house?"

"I didn't *expect* you to do anything different."

"Well then—"

"Just as I wouldn't *expect* you to do anything different if we were going out for a meal, or a film, or leaving for a holiday and already running late for our flight."

I thought about this. "No, I don't expect I would. Behave differently."

We were reaching a stand-off, I realised. One of the reasons I'd gone for Anna in the first place was that she always spoke her mind. This had a downside to it as well as an upside. I suppose all character traits do.

"Look," I said. "We talked about . . . all this when we first got together." Somehow, I couldn't say Susan's name at that moment.

"You talked. I listened. I didn't necessarily agree."

"Then you misled me."

"No, Paul, you didn't explain the full extent of it to me. Maybe in future when I get out my diary to write in a dinner date or a play or a weekend away, I should always add a note saying: subject to the extent of Susan Macleod's alcoholic intake."

"That's very unfair."

"It may be unfair but it also happens to be true."

We paused. It was a question of whether either of us wanted to take it further. Anna did.

"And while we're about it, Paul, I may as well say that Susan Macleod . . . is not really my kind of woman."

"I see."

"I mean, I shall always try to be kind to her for your sake."

"Yes, well, that's very generous of you. And while we're about it, I may as well say that I once promised her there would always be room in my life for her, even if it was just an attic."

"Paul, I don't want an attic in *my* life." And then she said it. "Especially not with a madwoman in it."

I let that last remark fill the silence that was growing between us. Eventually, no doubt sounding prim, I said, "I'm sorry you think she's mad."

She didn't withdraw her assertion. I realised that I was the only person in the world who understood Susan. And even if I'd moved out, how could I abandon her?

Anna and I continued for a few more weeks, each of us half-concealing our thoughts from the other. But I wasn't surprised when she bailed on the relationship. Nor, by then, did I blame her.

And so, by the end, you have tried soft love and tough love, feelings and reason, truth and lies, promises and threats, hope and stoicism. But you are not a machine, switching easily from one approach to another. Each strategy involves as much emotional strain on you as on her; perhaps more. Sometimes, when, lightly drunk, she is in one of her airy, exasperating moods, denying both reality and your concern for her, you find yourself thinking: she may be destroying herself in the long term, but in the short term, she's doing more damage to you. Helpless, frustrated anger overwhelms you; and, worst of all, righteous anger. You hate your own righteousness.

You remember the running-away fund she gave you when you were at university. You have never thought to make use of it before. Now, you take it all out, in cash. You go to a small, anonymous hotel towards the bottom of the Edgware Road, just up from Marble Arch. This is not a fashionable or expensive part of town. Next door is a small Lebanese restaurant. In the five days you are there, you do not drink. You want your mind to be lucid; you do not want either your anger or your self-pity to be exaggerated or distorted. You want your emotions to be whatever they are.

You remove a bunch of prostitutes' business cards from a nearby telephone box. They have been attached with Blu-Tack, and before laying them out on the small desk in your hotel room, you roll off the sticky little balls of adhesive and drop them in the wastepaper basket. You do this in a deliberate way. Then you lay the cards out like a game of patience and decide which of these glamorous women who do "hotel calls" you wish to fuck. You make your first phone call. The woman, naturally, looks nothing like the photo on the card. You note this, without caring, let alone protesting: on the scale of disappointment, this is nothing. The location and the transaction are the exact opposite of all you have previously imagined love and sex to be. Still, it is fine for what it is. Efficient, pleasurable, emotion-free; fine.

On the wall is a cheap print of a Van Gogh cornfield with crows. You enjoy looking at it: again, an efficient, second-rate, counterfeit pleasure. You think there is something to be said for the second-rate. Perhaps it is more reliable than the first-rate. For instance, if you were in front of the real Van Gogh, you might get nervous, be full of jacked-up expectations about whether or not you were reacting properly. Whereas no one—you, least of all—cares how you respond to a cheap print on a hotel wall. Perhaps that is how you should live your life. You remember, when you were a student, someone maintaining that if you lowered your expectations in life, then you would never be disappointed. You wonder if there is any truth in this.

When desire returns, you order up another prostitute. Later, you have a Lebanese dinner. You watch television. You lie on your bed, deliberately not thinking about Susan or anything to do with her. You do not care how anyone might judge you if they could see where you are and what you are doing. Doggedly, and almost without actual pleasure, you continue to spend your running-away fund until all that remains is enough for your bus fare back to SE15. You do not reproach yourself; nor do you experience guilt, now or later. You never tell anyone about this episode. But you begin to wonder—not for the first time in your life—if there is something to be said for feeling less.

THREE

He sometimes asked himself a question about life. Which are truer, the happy memories, or the unhappy ones? He decided, eventually, that the question was unanswerable.

He had kept a little notebook for decades now. In it he wrote down what people said about love. Great novelists, television sages, self-help gurus, people he met in his years of travelling. He assembled the evidence. And then, every couple of years or so, he went through and crossed out all the quotations he no longer believed to be true. Usually, this left him with only two or three temporary truths. Temporary, because the next time round, he would probably cross those out as well, leaving a different two or three now standing.

He had found himself on a train to Bristol the other day. Across the aisle was a woman with the *Daily Mail* spread out in front of her. He saw the bright headline, accompanied by a large photo. HEADMISTRESS, 49, SANK 8 GLASSES OF WINE, DROPPED CRISPS DOWN HER TOP, AND SAID TO PUPIL, "COME AND GET 'EM." After such a headline, what need to read the story?

And what chance of the reader finding a different moral to the one so fiercely implied? Any more than would have been the case, half a century previously, had the newspaper's hot moralism been applied to a story which, at the time, hadn't even made the local *Advertiser & Gazette.* For the next ten minutes and more he worked on the headline his own case might have elicited. He finally came up with: NEW BALLS, ANYONE? TENNIS CLUB SCANDAL AS HOUSEWIFE, 48, AND LONG-HAIRED STUDENT, 19, EXPELLED OVER RUMPY-PUMPY. As for the text below, it would write itself: "There were shock waves behind the lace curtains and laurel hedges of leafy Surrey last week as steamy allegations emerged of . . ."

Some people, when they grow old, decide to live by the sea. They watch the tides approach and recede, foam bubbling on the beach, further out the breakers, and perhaps, beyond all this, they hear the oceanic waves of time, and in such hinted outer vastness find some consolation for their own minor lives and impending mortality. He preferred a different liquid, with its own movements and its own destination. But he saw nothing eternal in it: just milk turning into cheese. He was suspicious of the grander view of things, and wary of indefinable yearnings. He preferred the daily dealings of reality. And he also admitted that his world, and his life, had slowly shrunk. But he was content with this.

For instance, he thought he probably wouldn't have sex again before he died. Probably. Possibly. Unless. But on balance, he thought not. Sex involved two people. Two persons, first person and second person: you and I, you and me. But nowadays, the raucousness of the first person within him was stilled. It was as if he viewed, and lived, his life in the third person. Which allowed him to assess it more accurately, he believed.

So, that familiar question of memory. He recognised that memory was unreliable and biased, but in which direction? Towards optimism? That made initial sense. You remembered your past in cheerful terms because this validated your existence. You didn't have to see your life as any kind of triumph—his own had hardly been that— but you did need to tell yourself that it had been interesting, enjoyable, purposeful. Purposeful? That would be pitching it a bit high. Still, an optimistic memory might make it easier to part from life, might soften the pain of extinction.

But you could equally argue the opposite. If memory is biased towards pessimism, if, retrospectively, all appears blacker and bleaker than it actually was, then this might make life easier to leave behind. If, like dear old Joan, dead now these thirty years and more, you had already been to hell and back in your lifetime, then what fear of actual hell, or, more probably, eternal nonexistence? There drifted into his mind words caught on the headcam of a British soldier in Afghanistan—words spoken by another soldier as he executed a wounded prisoner. "There you are. Shuffle off this mortal coil, you cunt," the man had said before pulling the trigger. Impressive to have Shakespeare half-quoted on the modern battlefield, he had thought at the time. Why had that come into his head? Perhaps Joan's swearing had been the connection. So he considered the upside to feeling that life was just a fucking coil to be shuffled off. And men were just cunts; not women, men. There might also be an evolutionary advantage to a pessimistic memory. You wouldn't mind making room for others in the food queue; you could see it as a social duty to wander off into the wilderness, or allow yourself to be staked out on some hillside for the greater good.

But that was theory; and here was practicality. As he saw it, one of the last tasks of his life was to remember her correctly. By which he didn't mean: accurately, day by day, year by year, from beginning to middle to end. The end had been terrible, and far too much middle had overhung the beginning. No, what he meant was this: it was his final duty, to both of them, to remember and hold her as she had been when they were first together. To remember her back to what he still thought of as her innocence: an innocence of soul. Before such innocence became defaced. Yes, that was the word for it: a scribbling-over with the wild graffiti of booze. Also, a losing of the face, and his subsequent inability to see her. To see, to recall what she had been like before he lost her, lost sight of her, before she disappeared into that chintz sofa—"Look, Casey Paul, I'm doing my disappearing act!" Lost sight of the first person—the only person—he had loved.

He had photographs, of course, and they helped. Smiling at him while leaning back against the trunk of a tree in some long-forgotten wood. Windswept on a broad empty beach with a row of shuttered huts in the distance behind her. There was even a picture of her in that tennis dress with the green trim. Photographs were useful, but somehow always confirmed the memory rather than liberating it.

He tried to get his mind to catch her on the wing. To remember her gaiety, her laughter, her subversiveness and her love for him, before everything became occluded. Her dashingness, and her gallant attempt to make happiness when the odds were always against her, always against them. Yes, this was what he was after: Susan happy, Susan optimistic, despite not having much of a clue what the future held. That was a talent, a lucky slice of her character. He himself tended to look at the future and decide from an assessment of probabilities whether optimism or pessimism was the appropriate outlook. He brought life to his temperament; she brought her temperament to life. It was more risky, of course; it brought more joy, but it left you no safety net. Still, he thought, at least they hadn't been defeated by practicality.

There was all this; and there was also the way she accepted him simply as he was. No, better: she enjoyed him as he was. And she had confidence in him: she looked at him and didn't doubt him; she thought he would make something of himself, and something of his life. Which in a sense he had done, though not as either of them would have foreseen.

She would say, "Let's pile all the Fancy Boys into the Austin and drive to the sea." Or to Chichester Cathedral, or Stonehenge, or a secondhand bookshop, or a wood with a thousand-year-old tree at the centre of it. Or to a horror flick, however much they scared the daylights out of her. Or to a funfair, where they would hurtle round the dodgems, stuff themselves with candyfloss, fail to dislodge coconuts from their holders and be whirled into the air by various devices until all the puff had gone out of them. He didn't know if he'd done all these things back then, with her; some perhaps later, some even with other people. But it was the kind of remembering he needed, and which brought her back even if she hadn't actually been there.

No safety net. One image would always recur, whenever he thought of her. He was holding her out of the window by her wrists, unable to pull her in or let her drop, both their lives in agonising stasis until something happened. And what *had* happened? Well, he had tried to organise people to pile mattresses high enough to break her fall; or, he had got the fire brigade to hold a jumping sheet; or . . . But they were locked together at the wrist like trapeze artists: he wasn't just holding her, she was holding him. And in the end his strength gave way, and he let her go. And though her fall was cushioned, it was still very grievous because, as she had once told him, she had heavy bones.

One entry in his notebook was, of course: "It is better to have loved and lost than never to have loved at all." That was there for a few years; then he crossed it out. Then he wrote it in again; then he crossed it out again. Now he had both entries side by side, one clear and true, the other crossed out and false.

When he thought back to life in the Village, he remembered it as being based on a simple system.

232

For each ailment, there was a single remedy. TCP for a sore throat; Dettol for a cut; Disprin for a headache; Vicks for chestiness. And beyond that lay greater matters but still with unitary solutions. The cure for sex is marriage; the cure for love is marriage; the cure for infidelity is divorce; the cure for unhappiness is work; the cure for extreme unhappiness is drink; the cure for death is a frail belief in the afterlife.

As an adolescent, he had longed for more complication. And life had let him discover it. At times, he felt he had had enough of life's complications.

A few weeks after his row with Anna he gave up his rented room and moved back to Henry Road. Somewhere, in some novel he subsequently read, he had come across the sentence: "He fell in love like a man committing suicide." It wasn't quite like that, but there was a sense in which he had no choice. He couldn't live with Susan; he couldn't establish a separate life away from her; therefore he went back to live with her. Courage or cowardice? Or mere inevitability?

At least by now he was familar with the patterned patternlessness of the life he was submitting to again. His reappearance was greeted not with happiness or relief, but with a blithe lack of surprise. Because such a return was always going to happen. Because young men must be allowed their delinquencies, but shouldn't be congratulated when they returned to a place they should never have left. He noted this discrepant reaction but didn't resent it; on the scale of things to be resented, it didn't really signify.

And so—for how long? another four, five years?—they continued under the same roof, with good days and bad weeks, swallowed rage, occasional outbursts and increasing social isolation. All this no longer made him feel interesting; instead, he felt a failure and an outcast. He never got close to another woman in this time. After a year or two, Eric could no longer stand the atmosphere, and moved out. The top two rooms were rented to nurses. Well, he couldn't get policemen.

But there was one discovery made during these years which surprised him, and which made his future life, when it came, easier. The office manager announced herself pregnant; they advertised for a stand-in, but could find no one suitable; he suggested himself for the job. It scarcely occupied the whole day, and he continued handling some legal aid cases. But he found the routine of admin, diary-keeping, mail, billings—even the banalities of maintaining the coffee machine and water cooler—gave him quiet satisfaction. In part, no doubt, because he often arrived from Henry Road in a state unfit for much more than low-level administration. But he also took unanticipated pleasure in running things. And his colleagues were straightforwardly grateful to him for making their lives easier. The contrast with Henry Road was blatant. When had Susan last thanked him for making her life less arduous than it would have been?

The office manager, with many explanations about the thrilling surprise of maternal love, announced that she wouldn't be returning. He took the job full-time; and, years later, this practical ability proved his means of escape. He managed offices for law firms, for charities, for NGOs, and so was able to travel, and move on when he needed to. He worked in Africa, and in North and South America. The routine satisfied a part of him he didn't know existed. He remembered how, back at the Village tennis club, he'd been shocked at the way some of the older members played. They were certainly competent, but inexpressive and uninventive, as if merely following the instructions of some long-dead coach. Well, that had been them, then. Now he could run an office—wherever, whenever—like any grooved old hacker. He kept his satisfactions to himself. And over the years he had also learned to see the point of money: what it could—and couldn't—do.

There was another thing. It was a job below his qualifications. Not that he didn't take it seriously;

he did. But since, professionally, he had now lowered his expectations, he found that he was rarely disappointed.

He had a duty to see back to how she had been, and to rescue her. But this wasn't just about her. He had a duty to himself. To see back and . . . rescue himself? From what? From "the subsequent wreckage of his life"? No, that was stupidly melodramatic. His life had not been wrecked. His heart, yes, his heart had been cauterised. But he had found a way to live, and continued with that life, which had brought him to here. And from here, he had a duty to see himself as he had once been. Strange how, when you are young, you owe no duty to the future; but when you are old, you owe a duty to the past. To the one thing you can't change.

He remembered, at school, being guided by masters through books and plays in which there was often a Conflict between Love and Duty. In those old stories, innocent but passionate love would run up against the duty owed to family, church, king, state. Some protagonists won, some lost, some did both at the same time; usually, tragedy ensued. No doubt in religious, patriarchal, hierarchical societies, such conflicts continued and still gave themes to writers. But in the Village? No church-going for his family. Not much of a hierarchical social structure, unless you counted the tennis and golf club committees, with their power to expel. Not much patriarchy, either—not with his mother around. As for family duty: he had felt no obligation to placate his parents. Indeed, nowadays the onus had shifted, and it was the parents' job to accept whatever "life choices" their child might make. Like running off to a Greek island with Pedro the hairdresser, or bringing home that gymslip-mother-to-be.

Yet this liberation from the old dogmas brought its own complexities. The sense of obligation became internalised. Love was a Duty in and of itself. You had a Duty to Love, the more so now that it was your central belief system. And Love brought many Duties with it. So, even when apparently weightless, Love could weigh heavily, and bind heavily, and its Duties could cause disasters as great as in the old days.

Another thing he had come to understand. He had imagined that, in the modern world, time and place were no longer relevant to stories of love. Looking back, he saw that they had played a greater part in his story than he ever realised. He had given in to the old, continuing, ineradicable delusion: that lovers somehow stand outside of time.

Now he was getting off the point. Susan and himself, all those years ago. There was her shame to deal with. But there was also, he knew, his shame.

An entry from his notebook which had survived several inspections: "In love, everything is both true and false; it's the one subject on which it's impossible to say anything absurd." He had liked this remark since first discovering it. Because for him it opened out into a wider thought: that love itself is never absurd, and neither are any of its participants. Despite all the stern orthodoxies of feeling and behaviour that a society may seek to impose, love slips past them. You sometimes saw, in the farmyard, improbable forms of attachment—the goose in love with the donkey, the kitten playing safely between the paws of the chained-up mastiff. And in the human farmyard, there existed forms of attachment which were just as unlikely; and yet never, to their participants, absurd.

One permanent effect of his exposure to the Macleod household had been a distaste for angry men. No, not distaste, disgust. Anger as an expression of authority, an expression of masculinity, anger as a prelude to physical violence: he hated it all. There was a hideous false virtue to anger: look at me, angry, look how I boil over because I am so filled with emotion, look how I am really alive (unlike all those cold fish over there), look how I am going to prove it by grabbing your hair and smashing your face into a door. And now look what you made me do! I'm angry about that too!

It seemed to him that anger was never just anger. Love was, usually, in itself, just love, even if it impelled some to behave in ways which made you suspect there was no love present anymore, and perhaps never had been. But anger, especially the sort which coated itself in self-righteousness (and perhaps all anger did) was so often an expression of something else: boredom, contempt, superiority, failure, hatred. Or even something apparently trivial, like a chafing dependence on female practicality.

Even so, and to his considerable surprise, he had finally stopped hating Macleod. True, the man was long dead—though it was perfectly possible, indeed reasonable, to hate the dead; and at one stage he imagined he would live with his hatred until the day he himself died. But it hadn't worked out that way.

He wasn't sure about the chronology of it all. At some point, Macleod had retired, but continued to live on in that large house, attended by a cook-housekeeper to whom he behaved with elaborate, antiquated politeness. Once a week he would go to the golf club and hit a stationary ball as if it were a personal enemy. He would garden furiously, smoke furiously, turn on the goggle-box and drink along to it until he could still just get himself to bed. Often the thieving Mrs. Dyer would find the blank-screened set still buzzing when she arrived.

Then, one winter morning, while he was planting out cabbages, Macleod had fallen to the hard ground and wasn't discovered for hours; the stroke had done its worst. Half-paralysed, but fully silenced, he now depended on regular visits from a nurse, monthly ones from his daughters, more erratic ones from Susan. Maurice, his old pal from *Reynolds News*, would drop by from time to time, and, in knowing contravention of medical advice, would pull out a half-bottle of whisky and pour some of it down Macleod's throat while the familiar eyes blinked back at him. By the time the housekeeper found him dead on the floor with the bedsheets wrapped round him, Susan had long since handed power of attorney to Martha and Clara. The house, with many unwanted contents, was sold to a dubious local who might have been fronting for a property developer.

Somewhere in this sequence, he had stopped hating Macleod. He didn't forgive him—he didn't consider forgiveness the opposite of hatred—but he acknowledged that his seething antipathy and nighttime rages had become somehow irrelevant. On the other hand, he didn't feel pity for Macleod, despite all the humiliations and infirmities visited upon him. These he regarded as inevitabilities; indeed, he nowadays regarded most things that happened as inevitabilities.

The question of responsibility? That seemed a matter for outsiders: only those with a sufficient lack of evidence and knowledge could confidently apportion blame. He was, even at this distance, still far too involved to do so himself. And he had also reached a stage in life where he had started pursuing counterfactuals. What if this had happened rather than that? It was idle but involving (and perhaps held the question of responsibility at bay). For instance, what if he hadn't been nineteen, with time on his hands and—while hardly aware of it—desperate for love when he had arrived at the tennis club? What if Susan, from religious or moral scruple, had discouraged his interest, and taught him nothing more than tactical astuteness when playing mixed doubles? What if Macleod had continued to hold a sexual interest in his wife? None of this might have happened. But given that it had, then if you wanted to attribute fault, you were straight away into prehistory, which now, in two of their three cases, had become inaccessible.

Those charged first few months had reordered his present and determined his future, even up to now. But what if, for instance, he and Susan hadn't been attracted to one another? What if one of their many cover stories had been true? He was a young man who drove her because she needed new glasses. He was a friend of one or both of the daughters. He was a kind of protégé of Gordon's. Now, in his state of slowly acquired calmness, he found he could easily imagine things other than they had been; the facts and feelings quite different.

Curious, he pursued this untaken path. For instance, he started helping Old Man Macleod with the gardening. As well as playing tennis with Susan, he took up golf, had lessons at the club and would often partner Gordon—as he'd been asked to call him—round the local eighteen holes when the dew still sparkled on the fairways. There was something about his presence which relaxed Old Man Macleod: that gruffness was only a mask, and Paul was able to help him relax a bit more on the tee; he even taught him (after flipping through an American golf manual) how to love that little dimpled ball rather than hate it. He—Casey Paul, as more than Susan now called him—discovered that he rather liked a drink: gin with Joan, beer with Gordon, an occasional glass of sherry with Susan; though all agreed that at a certain point enough was enough and one more was too many. And then—why not pursue this alternative life to, if not a logical, at least a conventional conclusion—what if he and one of the Macleod daughters became (as their parents would have put it) "sweet on one another"? Martha or Clara? Obviously Clara, who took more character traits from Susan. But this was counterfactual, and so he chose Martha.

The immediate consequence was that the Macleods did indeed come round to have sherry with his parents—an occasion he and Martha had been dreading, but which actually passed off quite well. The two couples were never going to make a harmonious bridge four, but there was nothing like fixing a date with the vicar of St. Michael's for everyone to overlook incompatibilities. And—since this counterfactual had now got way out of hand—he decided to decorate the wedding day with the most extravagantly beautiful weather, even unto a double rainbow. Then, on a whim, he chose to award himself the sister he never had. To stir things up a bit for his parents, he made her a lesbian. Oh, and she brought her baby along to the ceremony. The only baby in the Western world who didn't cry at an inappropriate moment during a wedding. Why not?

He shook his head to clear this strange vision that had come upon him. There were two ways of looking at life; or two extremes of viewpoint, anyway, with a continuum between them. One proposed that every human action necessarily carried with it the obliteration of every other action which might have been performed instead; life therefore consisted of a succession of small and large choices, expressions of free will, so that the individual was like the captain of some paddle steamer chugging down the mighty Mississippi of life. The other proposed that it was all inevitability, that prehistory ruled, that a human life was no more than a bump on a log which was itself being propelled down the mighty Mississippi, tugged and bullied, smacked and wheedled, by currents and eddies and hazards over which no control was possible. Paul thought it did not have to be one or the other. He thought a life—his own, of course—could be lived first under the dispensation of inevitability, and later under the dispensation of free will. But he also realised that retrospective reorderings of life are always likely to be self-serving.

On further thought, he decided that the unlikeliest part of his counterfactual was that Martha would ever have considered him a potential husband.

Did he feel regret at what he always thought of as his "handing back" of Susan? No: the proper word for that might be guilt; or its sharper colleague, remorse. But there was also an inevitability to it, which lent the action a different moral colouring. He found that he simply couldn't go on. He couldn't save her, and so he had to save himself. It was as simple as that.

No, of course it wasn't; it was much more

complicated. He could have gone on, both fooling and torturing himself. He could have gone on, calming her down and reassuring her even when her mind and memory ran in three-minute loops, from fresh surprise at his presence, even though he'd been sitting in the same chair for two hours, via rebuke for his nonexistent absence, through to alarm and panic, which he would quieten with soft talk and gentle memories that she would pretend to agree with even though she'd long ago drunk those memories clean out of her head. No, he could have gone on, acting as an emotional home help, watching over her progressive disintegration. But he would have had to be a masochist. And by that time he had made the most terrifying discovery of his life, one which probably cast a shadow over all his subsequent relationships: the realization that love, even the most ardent and the most sincere, can, given the correct assault, curdle into a mixture of pity and anger. His love had gone, had been driven out, month by month, year by year. But what shocked him was that the emotions which replaced it were just as violent as the love which had previously stood in his heart. And so his life and his heart were just as agitated as before, except that she was no longer able to assuage his heart. And that, finally, was when he had to hand her back.

He wrote a joint letter to Martha and Clara. He didn't go into emotional detail. He merely explained that he was obliged to travel on business for an extended period—perhaps several years—and would obviously not be able to take Susan with him. He would be leaving in three months, which he hoped would be enough time for them to make the appropriate arrangements. If, at some future point, it became necessary to put her into some kind of residential care, he would do what he could to help; though at present he was not in a position to contribute.

And most of this was true.

There was one visit he was obliged to make before going abroad. Was he dreading it or looking forward to it? Both, probably. It was five o'clock by the time he rang the bell, answered this time not by a counterpoint of yapping but by a single, distant bark. When Joan opened the door, there was a placid, elderly golden retriever beside her. She looked so foggy-eyed that it might as well have been a guide dog, he thought.

It was winter; Joan wore a tracksuit with a few cigarette burns on the bosom, and a pair of Russian house socks in which she padded along as softly as her dog. The sitting room mixed woodsmoke with cigarette smoke. The chairs were the same, but older; their occupants were the same, but older. The retriever, which answered to the name of Sibyl, panted from the journey to the front door and back.

"The yappers all died on me," Joan said. "Don't ever have dogs, Paul. They die on you, and then there comes a point when you don't know whether to get one last one or not. One for the road. So here we are, Sibyl and me. Either I'll die and break her heart or she'll die and break mine. Not much of a choice, is it? The gin's over there. Help yourself."

He did so, choosing the least filthy of the tumblers.

"So how are you keeping, Joan?"

"As you can see. Pretty much the same, except older, drunker, lonelier. How about you?"

"I'm thirty. I'm going abroad for a few years. Work. I've handed Susan back."

"Like a parcel? It's a bit fucking late, isn't it? Taking her back to the shop and asking for a refund?"

"It's not like that." He realised he might have some difficulty explaining to one drunk woman why he was leaving another.

"So how exactly is it?"

"It's like this. I tried to save her, I failed. I tried to stop her drinking, I failed. I don't blame her, it's way beyond that. And I remember what you told me back then—that she was more likely to get hurt than me. But I can't take it anymore. I can't face another ten days of it, let alone another ten years. So Martha's going to look after her. Clara refused, which surprised me. I said that . . .

247

if they needed to put her into a home at some point, I might be able to help. In the future. If I do well and make some money."

"You've certainly got it all worked out."

"It's self-protection, Joan. I couldn't take anymore."

"Girlfriend?" she asked, lighting another cigarette.

"I'm not that heartless."

"Well, finding another woman can bring an exceptional clarity of mind to a man all of a sudden. Remembering my own distant experiences of cock and cunt."

"I'm sorry it didn't work out for you, Joan."

"Your sympathy is about half a century too late, young man."

"I mean it," he said.

"And how do you think Martha will cope? Better than you? Worse? About the same?"

"I've no idea. And in a way I don't care. I don't care, otherwise I'll be dragged back into it all."

"It's not a question of getting dragged back. You're still in it."

"How do you mean?"

"You're still in it. You'll always be in it. No, not literally. But in your heart. Nothing ever ends, not if it's gone that deep. You'll always be walking wounded. That's the only choice, after a while. Walking wounded, or dead. Don't you agree?"

He looked across, but she wasn't addressing

him. She was addressing Sibyl, and patting her soft head. He didn't know what to say, because he didn't know if he believed her or not.

"Do you still cheat at the crossword?"

"You cheeky little bugger. But that's nothing new, is it?" He smiled at her.

He'd always liked Joan.

"And shut the door on your way out. I don't like to get up too many times in the course of a day."

He knew not to do anything like embrace her, so merely nodded, smiled and started to leave.

"Send a wreath when the time comes," she called after him.

He didn't know if she meant for her, or for Susan. Maybe even for Sibyl. Did dogs get wreaths? Another thing he didn't know.

What he didn't—or couldn't—tell Joan was his terrifying discovery that love, by some ruthless, almost chemical process, could resolve itself into pity and anger. The anger wasn't at Susan, but at whatever it was that had obliterated her. But even so, anger. And anger in a man caused him disgust. So now, along with pity and anger, he had self-disgust to deal with as well. And this was part of his shame.

He worked in a number of countries. He was in his thirties, then forties, perfectly presentable (as his mother would have put it), as well as solvent and not obviously mad. This was enough for him to find the sexual companionship, the social life, the daily warmth he needed—until he moved on to the next job, the next country, the next social circle, the next few years of being agreeable to and with new people, some of whom he might see in later years, some not. It was what he wanted; more to the point, it was all he felt able to sustain.

To some, his way of life might have sounded selfish, even parasitical. But he also took thought for others. He tried not to mislead, to exaggerate what was emotionally available. He didn't linger by jewellers' windows or go simperingly silent at photos of babies; nor did he claim he was looking to settle down, either with this person or indeed in this country. And—though it was a trait he didn't immediately identify—he was generally attracted to women who were . . . how to put it? Sturdy, independent and not obviously fucked-up. Women who had their own lives, who might enjoy his solid but passing presence as much as he did theirs. Women who wouldn't get too hurt when he moved on, and who wouldn't inflict too much pain if they were the first to jump.

He thought of this psychological pattern, this emotional strategy, as being honest and considerate, as well as necessary. He neither pretended nor offered more than he could deliver. Though of course, when he laid it all out like this, he saw that some might regard it as pure egotism. He also couldn't decide if his policy of moving on—from place to place, woman to woman—was courageous in admitting his own limitations, or cowardly in accepting them.

Nor did his new theory of living always work. Some women gave him thoughtful presents—and that scared him. Others, over the years, had called him a typical Englishman, a tightass, a cold fish; also, heartless and manipulative—though he believed his was the least manipulative approach to relationships that he knew. Still, it made some women cross with him. And on the rare occasions when he had tried to explain his life, his prehistory and the long-term state of his heart, the accusations sometimes became more pointed, and he was treated as if he had some infectious disease to which he should have admitted between the first and second dates.

But that was the nature of relationships: there always seemed to be an imbalance of one sort or another. And it was fine to plan an emotional strategy, but another thing when the ground opened up in front of you, and your defending troops toppled into a ravine which hadn't been marked on the map until a few seconds previously. And so there had been Maria, that gentle, calm Spanish woman who suddenly began making suicide threats, who wanted this, who wanted that. But he hadn't offered to be the father of her children—or anybody else's; nor did he intend to convert to Catholicism, even if that would have pleased her supposedly dying mother.

And then—since misunderstanding is democratically distributed—there had been Kimberly, from Nashville, who had so instantly fulfilled all his unwritten requirements—from laughing him into bed on the second date to embodying the very spirit of freehearted independence—that instead of quietly congratulating himself on his luck he had as near as dammit fallen smack into love with her. And at first she had rebuffed him with references to personal space and to "keeping things light." Yet this only made him the more desperate for her to move into his house that very afternoon, and he'd done stuff with flowers way beyond what he normally did, and found himself gazing at racks of diamond rings, and even dreaming of that perfect hideaway—perhaps an old trapper's shack (with full modern comforts, of course) up some tree-shadowed lane. He had offered marriage, and she had replied, "Paul, it doesn't work like that." When, in his delirium, she had patted his arm and said the kind of stuff he'd said to Maria, he heard himself accusing her of being selfish and manipulative and a cold fish and a typical

American woman—whatever he meant by that, as she was the first American woman he'd dated. So she ditched him by fax, and he got punitively drunk to the point of sudden rationality, when he fell into silly laughter, and a sense of the absurdity of all human dealings, and felt a sudden call for the monastic life, while also entertaining fantasies of Kimberly dressed as a nun and them having joyfully blasphemous sex, whereupon he booked two tickets for an early-morning flight to Mexico, but naturally overslept and the message on his answering machine when he woke was not from Kimberly but from the airline company telling him of his missed flight. Somehow he had got into work that day and gave a comic account of his misfortunes, which made his colleagues laugh, and made himself laugh, so that this lighter, distorted fiction swiftly took over from what had actually happened. And in later years he had silently thanked Kimberly for being smarter than he was—emotionally smarter. He had imagined that he'd learned a lot of emotional lessons from being with Susan. But maybe they were only emotional lessons about being with her.

He kept up with his men-friends when home on leave, or between jobs, over drinks or dinners which felt like sudden jerks of fast-forwarding. Some of them had turned into unremitting furrow-dwellers, and these were the ones who reminisced most sentimentally about the old days. Some were now on to second wives and stepchildren. One had turned gay, after all these years, having suddenly started noticing the napes of young men's necks. For a few, time brought no alteration. Bernard, red-faced and white-bearded, would give him a nudge, a head-toss and an overloud "Look at the arse on *that*," as a woman walked past their restaurant table. Bernard had been saying the same at twenty-five, though back then with an inaccurate American accent. Perhaps it was useful still to be reminded that some men mistook boorishness for honesty. Just as others mistook primness for virtue.

These intermittent friends were of different vintages: of the Fancy Boys, only Eric remained in his life. They were companionable for the necessary hours, and alcohol dissolved any distance between them. But in the way of things—or rather, in his way of things—he tended to remember mainly the phrases that either presumed or grated.

"Still in the game, eh, Paul?"

"Footloose and fancy-free?"

"Not found Miss Right yet? Or should I say Señorita Rita?"

"Do you think you'll ever settle down?"

"A pity you haven't had kids. You'd have made a good father."

"Never too late. Never say die, old chum."

"Yes, but don't forget: sperm degrades as we knock on."

"Don't you long for that little cottage with a blazing log fire and grandchildren on the knee?"

"He can't have grandchildren without having children first."

"You'd be amazed what medical science can do nowadays."

His occasional reappearances made some pleased with how their lives had turned out, and others, if not envious, a little restless. Then, in his fifties, he came home, moved to Somerset, and invested some of his savings.

"What gave you the idea of cheese?"

"Bad dreams for the rest of your life, old chum."

"Maybe there's a little dairymaid involved?"

"And look at the arse on *that*."

"Well, at least we'll be seeing more of you now."

But there was no dairymaid involved; and strangely, he didn't end up seeing more of his intermittent friends. Somerset could turn out to be as distant as Valparaiso or Tennessee, if you wanted things that way. And perhaps he chose to remember their heavy joshing because it helped keep them at bay just as he had kept his women friends at bay. Though now some were keeping themselves at bay, having reached the age when illness arrives. There were emails about prostate cancer, and back operations, and that little bit of heart trouble which maybe wasn't such good news. Vitamin pills and statins were consumed, while the World Service kept them company in their sleeplessness. And soon, no doubt, the funeral years would begin.

He remembered a friend he'd had, a lifetime back, at law college. Alan something. They hadn't kept up, for one reason or another. Alan had spent seven years training to be a vet, but on qualifying had immediately switched to the law.

One day, he'd asked his friend why he'd thrown up his first career so abruptly. Had he suddenly decided he didn't like animals? Was it the prospective hours? No, said Alan, none of that. He'd always thought it would be a good, purposeful job, helping to cure sick farmstock, bringing them either to safe birth or pain-free death, working outdoors, meeting all sorts of people. And it would have been all that, he knew. But what had finally put him off was a kind of squeamishness. He explained that if you spent several hours of the day with your arm up the backside of a cow, you couldn't help breathing in the animal's noxious exhalations. And that once they were inside you, they would inevitably seek to come back out again.

That was as far as Alan had gone. But he had naturally imagined Alan in bed with a girlfriend, and all going well between them, until some catastrophic buildup of cow gas hurtles from him, and the girl jumps from the bed, rushes for her clothes and is never seen again. Or perhaps this hadn't happened, but Alan couldn't bear to think of how it might be, if he was with someone he loved.

What had become of Alan? He had no idea. But Alan's story had stayed with him ever since. Because once you had been through certain things, their presence inside you never really disappeared. The cow gas would out, in one direction or another. Then you just had to live with the consequences until it dispersed. And yes, it had caused more than one girlfriend to run for her clothes, not just Anna. And no, at those times, he had not been much of a stoic.

In his youth, hot with pride at his love for Susan, he had been competitive, as all young men are. My cock is bigger than yours; my heart is bigger than yours. Young bucks boasting of their girlfriends' attributes. Whereas his boast had been: look how much more transgressive my relationship is than yours. And then, as well: look at the strength of my feelings for her, and hers for me. Which was what counted, obviously, because the strength of feeling governed the degree of happiness, didn't it? That had seemed blindingly logical to him at the time.

It used to be said that the Bhutanese were the happiest people on earth. In Bhutan there was little materialism, but a strong sense of kinship, society and religion. Whereas he lived in the materialistic West, where there was little religion and a weaker sense of both society and family. Did this give him an advantage, or a disadvantage?

More recently, the happiest people on earth were said to be the Danes. Not because of their supposed hedonism, but because of the modesty of their expressed hopes. Instead of aiming for the stars and the moon, their ambition was only to reach the next streetlamp and, being pleased when they did so, were the happier for it. He remembered again that woman, somebody's girlfriend, who said that she had lowered her expectations because this made you less likely to be disappointed. And therefore more happy? Was this what it was like to be Danish?

As for whether strength of feeling correlated to degree of happiness, his own experience now led him to doubt it. You might as well say, the more you ate, the better your digestion; or, the faster you drove, the quicker you got there. Not if you drove into a brick wall. He remembered that time, out in his Morris Minor with Susan, when the accelerator cable had broken, or jammed, or whatever. They were certainly roaring away up that hill, until he had the wit to disengage the clutch. He'd been doing two things at the same time: panicking and thinking clearly. That's how his life had been, back then. Nowadays, he always thought clearly; but occasionally, he found he missed the panic.

And here was another factor, whether you were Bhutanese, Danish or British. If the statistics of happiness depend on personal reporting, how can we be sure that anyone is as happy as they claim to be? What if they aren't telling the truth? No, we have to assume that they are, or at least that the testing system allows for lying. So the real question lay beneath: assuming that those canvassed by anthropologists and sociologists are reliable witnesses, then surely "being happy" is the same as "reporting yourself happy"? Whereupon any subsequent objective analysis—of brain activity, for instance— becomes irrelevant. To say sincerely that you are happy is to be happy. At which point, the question disappears.

And if that was so, then perhaps the argument could be extended. For example, to say that you had once been happy, and to believe what you were saying, was the same as actually to have been happy. Could that be true? No, that was surely specious. On the other hand, the emotional record was not like a history book; its truths were constantly changing, and true even when incompatible.

For instance, he had noticed during his life one difference between the sexes in the reporting of relationships. When a couple broke up, the woman was more likely to say, "It was all fine until *x* happened." The *x* being a change of circumstances or location, the arrival of an extra child, or, all too often, some routine—or not so routine—infidelity. Whereas the man was more likely to say, "I'm afraid it was all wrong from the start." And he would be referring to a mutual incompatibility, or a marriage made under duress, or an unrevealed secret on one or both sides, which had later emerged. So she was saying, "We were happy until," while he was saying, "We were never really happy." And when he had first noticed this discrepancy, he had tried to work out which of them was more likely to be telling the truth; but now, at the other end of his life, he accepted that both were doing so. "In love, everything is both true and false; it's the one subject on which it's impossible to say anything absurd."

When he bought a half-share in the Frogworth Valley Artisanal Cheese Company, he had imagined himself as a kind of owner-manager. Co-owner–co-manager. He had a desk and a chair and a rather decrepit computer terminal; he also had his own white coat, though was rarely required to put it on. Hillary ran the office. He had imagined himself running Hillary; but she didn't need running. He offered to help out and muck in; though mainly he watched things happen around him, and smiled. When Hillary went on holiday, he was allowed to take over her desk.

Where he proved most useful to the company (which only consisted of five people) was stall-holding at farmers' markets. It wasn't easy to find someone regular, and Barry, who'd done it for years, was growing unreliable. He was happy to stand in when required. Driving to one of the nearby towns, setting up the stall, laying out the cheeses, their captions, the tasting plates, the plastic cup of toothpicks. He wore a tweed cap and a leather apron, but knew he hardly passed for Somerset born-and-bred. Behind him was a plastic backdrop bearing a colour photograph of happy goats. The other stall-holders were friendly; he would swap two fivers for a tenner, two tenners for a twenty. He explained to customers the age of the cheeses and their characteristics: this one rolled in ash, this in chives, this in crushed chillis. He enjoyed doing all this. It gave him the level of social inter-action he required nowadays: cheerful, mutually sustaining, with no question of intimacy—even if he did sometimes flirt lightly with Betty of Betty's Best Home-Made Pies. It passed the time. Ah, that phrase. A sudden memory of Susan talking about Joan. "We're all just looking for a place of safety. And if you don't find one, then you have to learn how to pass the time." Back then, it had sounded like a counsel of despair; now, it struck him as normal, and emotionally practical.

Despite having no expectation of, nor desire for, some final relationship—or perhaps because of this—he often found himself drawn to all those public displays of wantingness. The personal ads, the "soulmates" columns, the TV dating shows, and those newspaper features where couples go for a meal, mark one another out of ten, report on or confess to inept chopstick behaviour, and then answer (or not) the question of whether they had kissed. "A quick hug" or "Only on the cheek" were frequent responses. Some blokes would answer smugly, "A gentleman never tells." It was meant to sound sophisticated, but showed far too much class deference: "gentlemen," in his experience, were as boastful as any other males. Still, he followed all these brave, tentative forays of the heart with a mixture of tenderness and scepticism. He hoped it might work out for them, even as he doubted that it would.

"A gentleman never tells." Well, it might occasionally be true. For instance, Uncle Humphrey, stinking of booze and cigars, coming into Susan's bedroom to demonstrate "a party kiss," and then demanding one (or more) on an annual basis. He doubted Uncle Humph had "told." But this hardly made him a "gentleman"—quite the opposite. Uncle Humph, whose lechery had resulted in Susan not believing in the afterlife. Had his behaviour affected her in other ways? Impossible to tell, at this distance. And so he dismissed that long-dead uncle from his mind.

He preferred to remember Joan. He wished he'd known her as a bounding tennis champion, then as a girl who went off the rails, then as a kept woman. Was the man who kept her, and then dismissed her, a "gentleman"? Susan had withheld his name, and there was no finding it now.

He smiled at the thought of Joan. He remembered the yappers, and Sibyl, the elderly golden retriever. Which of them had died first, Joan or Sibyl? She'd asked him to send flowers. Though for whom was never made clear. Whenever he'd been tempted to get a dog, he heard Joan's warning voice about them dying on you. So he never got a dog. Nor was he ever tempted to do crosswords or drink gin.

"Little man, you've had a busy day."

This is the greeting she often sings at you, when you visit her on home leaves.

Except when it is:

"Clap hands, here comes Charlie,
Clap hands, good time Charlie,
Clap hands, here comes Charlie now."

Martha, to your continuing surprise, never objects to your visits, and never asks you for money. She looks after her mother herself, with an occasional nurse in attendance. You get the impression that Martha's husband is doing well in . . . whatever he does. She told you once, which means you can no longer ask.

Susan's mind has slipped a little more each time you see her. Short-term memory disappeared a while ago, and long-term memory is a shifting, blurry palimpsest from which clear but unconnected phrases will occasionally be picked out by her fading brain. What often rises to the surface are songs and catchphrases from decades previously.

"High o'er the fence leaps Sunny Jim,
Force is the food that raises him."

Some advertising jingle for a breakfast cereal—from her own childhood? from that of her children? In your house, you had Weetabix.

She has long ago ceased to drink; indeed, she has forgotten that she was ever a drinker. She seems to know that you are, or were, something in her life, but not that she once loved you, and

264

you loved her in return. Her brain is ragged, but her mood is strangely stable. The panic and pandemonium have drained out of her. She is alarmed by neither your arrival nor your departure. Her manner is satirical at times, disapproving at others, but always a little superior, as if you aren't a person of much consequence. You find all this agonising, and try to resist the temptation to believe that you deserve what you are getting.

"He's a dirty stop-out, that one," she will confide to the nurse in a stage whisper. "I could tell you things about him that would make your hair stand on end."

The nurse looks at you, so you shrug and smile, as if to say, "What can you do, it's so sad, isn't it?" while realizing that even now you are betraying her, even in this new and last extremity of hers. Because she could, of course, tell the nurse a thing or two about you, and the nurse's hair might well stand on end.

You remember her saying that she wasn't afraid of death, and that her only regret would be over not knowing what happened afterwards. But now she has very little past and—literally—no thought for the future. She has only a ghostplay on some frayed screen of memory, which she takes to be the present.

"*You're* a played-out generation."

"Got to eat a peck of dirt before you die."

"Clap hands, here comes . . . Sunny Jim."
"One of the worst criminals in the world."
"Where've you been all my life?"
At least, you think, there is something of her still left among these shreds and patches.

> "Oh dear, what can the matter be?
> Three old ladies got locked in the la-va-
> tree,
> They were there from Monday to
> Saturday,
> Reading the *Radio Times.*"

Yes, you remember teaching her that one. So at least she hasn't turned into an entirely different person. You've heard about that happening: pillars of the church screaming obscenities, sweet old ladies turning into Nazis, and so on. But this is faint comfort. Perhaps, if she became unrecognizable and slipped completely out of character, it would all be less painful to deal with.

Once—and naturally in front of the nurse—she dredges up a football song which can only have come from you:

> "If I had the wings of a sparrow,
> If I had the arse of a crow,
> I'd fly over Tottenham tomorrow,
> And shit on the bastards below."

But the nurse has, of course, heard far worse in her years of caring for the elderly and demented, so she merely cocks an eyebrow at you and asks,

"Chelsea supporter?"

What makes it unbearable, what makes you so exhausted and depressed after twenty minutes in her presence that you want to run outside and howl, is this: though she can't name you, never asks you any questions or answers any of yours, she still, at one level, registers your presence and responds to it. She doesn't know who the fuck you are, or what you do, or even your fucking name, but at the same time, she recognises you, and judges you morally and finds you wanting. It is this which urges you to run out of the house and howl; and this which makes you realise that, perhaps at some similar unconscious level, in some remote part of your brain, you still love her. And because this awareness is unwelcome, it makes you want to howl the more.

And while he was tormenting himself, here was a question he would often arrive at when his mind followed a particular trail of memory. Handing back Susan had been an act of self-protection on his part. There was no doubt about that; and no doubt in his mind that he had to do it. But beyond this, was it an act of courage, or of cowardice?

And if he couldn't decide, perhaps the answer was: both.

• • •

But she had marked his life in so many ways, some for the better, some the worse. She had made him more generous and open to others though also more suspicious and enclosed. She had taught him the virtue of impulsiveness; but also its dangers. So he had ended up with a cautious generosity and a careful impulsiveness. His pattern of life for twenty years and more had been a demonstration of how to be impulsive and careful at the same time. And his generosity to others also came, like a pack of bacon, with a "use by" date on it.

He always remembered what she had said to him after they left Joan's house that day. Like most young men, especially those first in love, he had viewed life—and love—in terms of winners and losers. He, obviously, was a winner; Joan, he assumed, had been a loser, or, more likely, not even a competitor. Susan had put him right. Susan had pointed out that everyone has their love story. Even if it was a fiasco, even if it fizzled out, never got going, had all been in the mind to begin with: that didn't make it any the less real. And it was the only story.

At the time, he had been sobered by her words, and Joan's story had made him think of her quite differently. Then, over the years, as his life developed, as caution and carefulness began to predominate, he realised that he, no less than

Joan, had had his love story, and perhaps there wasn't another one to come. So now he better understood how couples clung to their own story—each, often, to a separate part of it—long after it had gone cold on them, even to the point where they were not sure they could bear one another. Bad love still contained the remnant, the memory, of good love—somewhere, deep down, where neither of them any longer wanted to dig.

He found himself often wondering about other people's love stories; and sometimes, because he was a calm and unintimidating presence, they would confide in him. Mostly, it was women who did so, but that was unsurprising; men—himself a prime example—were both more covert and less eloquent. And even when he guessed that the love stories of the misled and the forsaken had become a little less authentic with each retelling—that such tales were the equivalent of Winston Churchill in an Aylesbury backstreet, all rouged and made up for the Pathé News camera—even if this was the case, he was still moved. Indeed, he was more moved by the lives of the bereft and the unchosen than he was by stories of success in love.

On the one hand, there were the furrow-dwellers, tunnelling deeper into the earth, and who, understandably, were not communicative about their inner selves. And at the other extreme were those who would tell you their entire lives, their only story, either in a series of outpourings, or in a single episode. Where had he been that time? He could see the beachfront bar with its silly cocktails, feel the warm night breeze, hear the thudding backbeat from tinny loudspeakers. He was at ease with the world, watching other people's lives develop. No, that was too grand a way of putting it: he was observing the young get cheerfully drunk and turn their minds to sex, romance and something more. But though he was indulgent—even sentimental—about the young, and protective of their hopes, there was one scene he was superstitious about, and preferred not to witness: the moment when they flung away their lives because it just felt so right—when, for instance, a smiling waiter delivered a mound of mango sorbet with an engagement ring glittering in its domed apex, and a bright-eyed proposer fell to bended knee in the sand . . . The fear of such a scene would often lead him to an early night.

So he was sitting at the bar, halfway through his third and theoretically final cigarette of the evening, when a man in beach shorts and flip-flops climbed onto the stool beside him.

"Mind if I bum one?"

"Be my guest." He passed across the pack, then some hotel book-matches with a palm tree on the cover.

"Smokers, we're a dying breed, right?"

The fellow was probably in his forties, as lightly drunk as he was, English, genial, unpushy. None of that fake bonhomie you sometimes encountered, the assumption that you must have more in common than you did. And so they sat there quietly, smoking away, and maybe the lack of false small talk encouraged the man to turn and announce in a level, meditative tone,

"She said she wanted to rest on my shoulder as lightly as a bird. I thought that sounded poetic. Also, bloody brilliant, just what a fellow needs. Never went for clingy."

The man paused. Paul was always happy to supply a prompt.

"But it didn't work out?"

"Two problems." The fellow inhaled, then blew the smoke into the scented air. "Number one, birds fly away, don't they? That's in their nature, as a bird, isn't it? And number two, before they do, they always shit on your shoulder."

And with that he stubbed out his cigarette, nodded and walked off down the beach towards the gentle tide.

It came into his head, in one of those whimsical, sentimental moods he always sought to guard against, to try and make one of Susan's famous upside-down cakes. Over the years, he had become a competent baker, and so imagined that he could work out what had gone wrong. Too much fruit, too little baking powder, too much flour—that was his best guess.

The mixture certainly looked surly and unpromising in the tin. But when he opened the oven door, it had surprisingly risen to its correct height, the fruit looked evenly distributed, and it smelt like . . . cake. He let it cool, then cut himself a small slice. It tasted fine. Eating it failed to set off any specific memories, for which he was grateful. He was also grateful that he wasn't able to repeat someone else's mistakes, only his own.

He cut himself another slice and then, suddenly suspicious of his own motives, threw the rest in the bin. He turned on Wimbledon and watched as two tall, baseball-capped men hit aces past one another for game after game. He chewed his cake and wondered idly what might happen if he went back to the Village and presented himself at the tennis club. Applied for membership. Asked to play in, even at his advanced age. The bad boy returned: the Village's own John McEnroe. No, that was another sentimentality. Doubtless there would be no one left who remembered him. Or, more likely, all he would find would be a neat little housing estate. No, he would never go back. He was deeply incurious about whether his parents' house, or the Macleods', or Joan's, were still standing. Those places would hold no emotions for him at this distance. That's what he told himself, anyway.

Towards the end of Wimbledon fortnight, the broadcasters showed more doubles matches: men's, women's, mixed. Naturally, he was most interested in the mixed. "The most vulnerable spot is always down the middle, Casey Paul." Not anymore: the players were so fit, so quick and solid on the volley, and their rackets had sweet spots the size of their heads. Another change was the lack of chivalry, certainly at this level. As he remembered it, back in the day, male players would hit as hard as possible against the opposing man, but when rallying with a woman would hold back on the power, and rely more on a change of angle or depth; maybe throw in a slice or a drop shot. It was a bit more than chivalry, in fact: it was simply boring to watch a man outhitting and overpowering a woman.

He hadn't played tennis for years; decades indeed. When he lived in the States, a temporary friend had introduced him to golf. At first this felt an ironic surprise; but it was absurd to hold a prejudice against a game just because Gordon Macleod had once played it. He came to know the joy of a perfect contact between club and ball, the shame of a shank; and to appreciate the strategic intricacies of tee to green. Nevertheless, as he took aim down a fairway, his head properly filled with the coach's advice about taking the club back, use of the hips and legs, and the importance of the follow-through, he did occasionally hear, as if in a whisper, the sweet, laughing opinion of Susan Macleod that it was plain unsporting to hit a stationary ball.

Gordon Macleod: whom he had once wanted to kill, even if Joan had told him there hadn't been a local murder since the Villagers wore woad. An exemplar of the kind of Englishman he most loathed. Patronising, patriarchal, manneredly precise. Not to mention violent and controlling. He remembered how it had seemed to him that Macleod was somehow preventing him from growing up: not by doing anything, simply by existing. "And how many Fancy Boys are you providing yourself with this weekend?" Bravely, Susan had responded, "I think it's just Ian and Eric this weekend. Unless the others turn up as well." Gordon Macleod's words had been like fire; he'd laughed at them, as Susan had done, but they had scorched his skin.

And then there was that other occasion when words were spoken which had echoed down his life. That furious, squat man in his dressing gown, his eyes invisible in the gloom, bullying down on him as he gripped the banister in panic.

"Whatski? Whatski, my fine and feathered friend?"

At the time, he had blushed, feeling his skin burn. But beyond this, he thought the fellow must simply be mad. That's to say, mad enough to have somehow listened in to his and Susan's private conversations. Unless he'd hidden a tape recorder beneath his wife's bed. And the thought of that had made him blush all over again.

It had taken him years to realise that this had not been crazy malevolence, but something quite unintended, which nevertheless held a powerful and destructive resonance. Gordon Macleod, roused from his bed by the sound of his wife's lover, had merely, in that moment, and probably with no ulterior motive, fallen back on the private language he had shared with Susan. Shared? More than that—created. And which Susan had then brought into her relationship with him. Unthinkingly. You say "darling," you say "my love," you say "kiss me hardly," you say "whatski?," you say "my fine and feathered friend," because those are the words which come to you at that moment. With no ulterior motive on her part either. And now he wondered if any of her turns of phrase, which had so beguiled him, had been her own. Perhaps only "We're a played-out generation," because it seemed unlikely that Gordon Macleod, in all his self-importance, believed that he and men of his age were played out.

He remembered a public service advertisement from the time when the government, grudgingly, had acknowledged the existence of AIDS. There were two versions of the ad, he seemed to

275

remember: a photo of a woman in bed with about half a dozen men, and one of a man in bed with about half a dozen women, all side by side like sardines. The text pointed out that every time you went to bed with someone new, you also went to bed with everyone he or she had previously gone to bed with. The government had been talking about sexually transmitted disease. But it was the same with words: they too could be sexually transmitted.

And actions as well, for that matter. Except that—strangely, fortunately—actions had never caused a problem. He had never found himself thinking, Oh, when you did that with your hand or arm or leg or tongue, you must also have done it with x and y and z. Such thoughts and images had never bothered him, and he was grateful, because he could easily imagine how ghostly antecedents in your head could drive you mad. But ever since Gordon Macleod's sneer had first made sense to him, he had become conscious— at times, absurdly so—of what must have been going on, verbally, since the day Adam or Eve or whoever it might have been first took another lover.

Once, he had mentioned this discovery to a girlfriend: lightly, almost frivolously, as if it were natural and inevitable and therefore *interesting*. A day or two later, in bed, she had teasingly called him "my fine and feathered friend."

"No!" he had shouted, instantly retreating to his side of the mattress, "You're not allowed to call me that!"

She had been shocked by his vehemence. And he had shocked himself. But he was protecting a phrase which had always been uniquely between Susan and himself. Except that, earlier, it had been a phrase uniquely between the newly married Mr. Gordon Macleod and his hopeful, puzzled wife.

So, for a while—say, twenty years or more—he had found himself morbidly sensitive to lovers' language. This was ridiculous, of course. He saw rationally that there was only a limited vocabulary available, and it shouldn't matter when the same words were recycled, when nightly, across the globe, billions asserted the uniqueness of their love with secondhand phrases. Except that sometimes it did. Which meant that here, as elsewhere, prehistory ruled.

He imagined the Village tennis courts replaced by a spread of the finest modern boxes, or perhaps a more lucrative clump of low-rise flats. He wondered if anyone, anywhere, had ever looked at a housing development and thought: Why don't we knock them all down and build a nice tennis club, one with the latest all-weather courts? Or maybe—yes, why don't we go further and lay some proper old-fashioned grass courts, for tennis as it once used to be? But no one would ever do, or even think, that, would they? Things, once gone, can't be put back; he knew that now. A punch, once delivered, can't be withdrawn. Words, once spoken, can't be unsaid. We may go on as if nothing has been lost, nothing done, nothing said; we may claim to forget it all; but our innermost core doesn't forget, because we have been changed forever.

Here was a paradox. When he had been with Susan, they had scarcely discussed their love, analysed it, sought to understand its shape, its colour, its weight and its boundaries. It was simply there, an inevitable fact, an unshakeable given. But it was also the case that neither of them had the words, the experience, the mental equipment to discuss it. Later, in his thirties and forties, he had gradually acquired emotional lucidity. But in these later relationships of his, he had felt less deeply, and there was less to discuss, so his potential articulacy was rarely required.

He had read, some years before, that a common psychological trope in men's attitude to women was the "rescue fantasy." Perhaps it stirred in them memories of fairy tales in which valiant knights came across pretty maidens locked in towers by wicked guardians. Or those classical myths in which other maidens—usually naked—

were chained to rocks for the sole purpose of being rescued by dauntless warriors. Who usually discovered a convenient sea serpent or dragon which had to be eliminated first. In modern, less mythical times, it appeared that the woman about whom men most had rescue fantasies was Marilyn Monroe. He had viewed this sociological datum with a degree of scepticism. Odd how rescuing her seemed inevitably to involve sleeping with her. Some rescue that would prove. Whereas in fact, as it seemed to him, the most effective way to rescue Marilyn Monroe would have been *not* to sleep with her.

He didn't think that, as a nineteen-year-old, he had been suffering from a rescue fantasy with Susan. On the contrary, he suffered from a rescue reality. And unlike maidens in towers or chained to rocks, who attracted a whole swirl of knights looking for chivalric action, and unlike Marilyn Monroe, whom every Western man dreamed of liberating (if only to lock her up in a tower of his own making), in the case of Susan Macleod, there was not a great queue of knights, cinemagoers and Fancy Boys squabbling for the right to rescue her from her husband. He had believed he could save her; further, that *only* he could save her. That was no fantasy; it was practicality and brute necessity.

At this distance, he realised, he no longer had a memory of Susan's body. Of course, he remembered her face, and her eyes and her mouth and her elegant ears, and what she looked like in her tennis dress; there were photographs to confirm all this. But a sexual memory of her body: that had gone. He couldn't remember her breasts, their shape, their fall, their firmness or otherwise. He couldn't remember her legs, what form they took, and how she parted them and what she did with them when they made love. He couldn't remember her undressing. It was as if she'd undressed as women did on the beach, with lots of prim ingenuity beneath a capacious towel, but emerging in a nightdress rather than a swimming costume. Had they always made love with the lights out? He couldn't remember. Perhaps he'd closed his eyes a lot.

She had a corset, that he remembered; well, doubtless several. Which had—whatever they were called—straps for holding up her stockings. Suspenders, that was it. How many per leg? Two, three? But he knew she only ever attached the front one. This private eccentricity came back to him now. As for what her bras had been like . . . At nineteen, he didn't have the slightest underwear fetishism, any more than she took an erotic interest in his vests and pants. He couldn't even remember what his pants had looked like at that age. He'd had a period of wearing string vests, which for some reason he had imagined to be cool.

She had no coquetry about her, that was certain. No flirty bits of flesh showing. How did they kiss? He couldn't even remember that: Whereas, with later, lesser attachments, there were astonishing moments of sexual freeze-frame still in his head. Maybe, as you got better at sex, the sex became more memorable. Or maybe, the deeper your feelings, the less the particulars of sex mattered. No, neither of these were true. He was just trying to find a theory to explain an oddity.

He remembered when she had told him, just like that, how many times they had made love. A hundred and fifty-three, or some such number. Back then, it had thrown him into all sorts of pondering. Should he have been counting too? Was it a lapse in love that he wasn't, or hadn't? And so on. Now, he thought: a hundred and fifty-three, the number of times he had come up to that point. But what about her? How many orgasms had she had? Indeed, did she ever have one? There was pleasure and intimacy, surely; but orgasm? At the time he couldn't tell, nor did he ask; nor know how to ask. To put it more truthfully, he had never thought of asking. And now it was too late.

He tried to imagine why she might have decided to count. To begin with, as a matter of pride and attentiveness, in bed with only the second lover of her life, and that after a long drought. But then he remembered the anguished whisper of her plea, "Don't give up on me just yet, Casey Paul." So maybe counting had turned from a matter of acclaim to one of anxiety and dismay: the fear that he might leave her, the fear that she might never have another lover. Was that it? He gave up. He stopped examining the past, chasing down what Joan had memorably called "my own distant experiences of cock and cunt."

One evening, glass in hand, he was idly following the televised highlights of the Brazilian Grand Prix. He wasn't much interested in the bland plutocracy of Formula One; but he did like to watch young men taking risks. In that respect, the race was gratifying. Heavy rain had made the track dangerous; pools of standing water sent even former world champions aquaplaning smack into the barriers; the race was stopped twice, and frequently brought under the control of the safety car. Everyone drove cautiously, except for nineteen-year-old Max Verstappen of the Red Bull team. He overtook his way from almost last place to third, making moves his elders and supposed betters declined to dare. The commentators, astonished by this display of skill and guts, sought explanation. And one of them provided it: "They say your risk profile doesn't stabilise until you're about twenty-five."

This statement made him attend even more

closely. Yes, he thought: a treacherous circuit, visibility reduced by spray to almost zero, others trepidatious while you felt invulnerable, going flat out thanks to a risk profile as yet unstabilised. Yes, he remembered that all too well. It was called being nineteen. And some would crash and some wouldn't. Verstappen hadn't. So far, anyway: though he had another six years to go before neurophysiology rendered him entirely sensible.

But if Verstappen was showing youthful fearlessness rather than true courage, did the same age disclaimer apply in reverse: to cowardice? He'd certainly been under twenty-five when he committed an act of cowardice which had haunted him all his life. He and Eric were staying at the Macleods', and had gone off to a funfair in a hilly park. They were walking down from the top, side by side, chatting, and failed to notice a group of youths coming up towards them. As they drew level, one leaned into Eric with his shoulder, spinning him round; another tripped him, and a third went in with his boot. He took all this in with a kind of heightened peripheral vision—how long before Eric was on the ground? a second? two?—and had instantly, instinctively run away. He kept saying to himself, "Find a policeman, find a policeman," but even as he did so, he knew that wasn't the reason he was running. He was afraid of getting beaten up himself. The rational part of him knew that policemen were a rare sight at funfairs. So he ran to the bottom of the hill on this futile, pretend quest, without actually asking anyone where he might find help. Then he walked back up, nauseous at what he might find. Eric was on his feet, blood on his face, feeling his ribs. He could no longer remember what had been said—whether he offered his fake excuse—and they drove back to the Macleod house. Susan bandaged Eric, with liberal use of Dettol, and insisted he stay until the bruising had gone down and the cuts mended. Which Eric had done. Neither then nor later had Eric rebuked him for cowardice, or asked why he'd disappeared.

You could get through a life, if you were careful, and lucky, without having your courage much tested—or rather, your cowardice revealed. That time Macleod had attacked him in the book room he'd certainly run for it, after throwing one ineffective punch in reply to Macleod's three. And when he'd scuttled out of the back door, he hadn't been trying to find a policeman, either. He had made the probably correct calculation that Macleod was drunk enough and angry enough to go on attempting to hit him until he succeeded. Despite being younger, and reasonably fit, he hadn't fancied his chances at close quarters. It wasn't like facing an under-12, under-6-stone schoolboy of equal timorousness.

And then again, more recently. "Recently" in the sense of "fifteen or twenty years ago." That was how the mind, and time, worked nowadays. He'd been back in England for only a few years. He'd visited Susan a couple of times, bringing no visible pleasure or benefit to either of them. One evening, the phone rang. It was Martha Macleod, now—for a long time—Mrs. Something-or-Other.

"My mother has been temporarily sectioned" was her opening line.

"I'm very sorry to hear that."

"She's in . . ." and cited the mental health department of a local hospital. He knew its reputation. A doctor friend, with professional dryness, had once told him, "You have to be *really* mad to get in there."

"Yes."

"It's a terrible place. It's like Bedlam. Lots of people screaming. Either that or they're zombified with tranquillizers."

"Yes." He didn't ask which category Susan was in.

"Would you go and see her? And see the place?"

He thought: this is the first time in a quarter of a century that Martha has asked anything of me. Disapproval at first; quiet superiority thereafter; though she had always been polite to him. She must be at the end of her tether, he thought. Well, he had been there in his time too; and knew how elastic the end of a tether could be. So he considered her request.

"Maybe." He was going up to town in a couple of days, as it happened. But he wasn't going to tell her that.

"I think it would do her good to see you. In the place she's in."

"Yes."

He'd left it like that. After he put the phone down, he thought: I looked after her for years. I tried my best. I failed. I handed her over to you. So it's your turn now.

But he didn't believe his own bitter logic. It was like saying, "Find a policeman, find a policeman." The truth was, he couldn't face it: he couldn't face seeing her, the remnant of her, whether screaming or zombified, among the screaming and zombified. He tried to think of his decision as an act of necessary self-protection; also, protection of the picture he had of her in his head. But he knew the truth. He was scared of going there.

As he grew older, his life turned into an agreeable routine, with enough human contact to sustain and divert, but not disturb, him. He knew the contentment of feeling less. His emotional life was recast as a social life. He was on nodding and smiling terms with many, as he stood in his leather apron and tweed cap in front of a colour photograph of happy goats. He prized stoicism and calm, which he had achieved less through some exercise of philosophy, more from a slow growth within him; a growth like coral, which in most weathers was strong enough to keep out the ocean breakers. Except when it wasn't.

So his life consisted mainly of observation and memory. It was not a bad mix. He viewed with distaste those men in their sixties and seventies who carried on behaving as if they were in their thirties: a whirl of younger women, exotic travel and dangerous sports. Fat tycoons on yachts with hairy arms round thin models. Not to mention respectable husbands who, in a turmoil of existential anguish and Viagra, left their wives of several decades. There was a German expression for this fear, one of those concertina words the language specialised in, which translated as "the panic at the shutting of the doors." He himself felt untroubled by that shutting; though he saw no reason to hurry it up.

He knew what they said of him locally: Oh, he likes to keep himself to himself. The phrase was descriptive, not judgemental. It was a principle of life the English still respected. And it wasn't just about privacy, about an Englishman's home—even a pebbledash semi—being his castle. It was about something more: about the self, and where you kept it, and who, if anyone, was allowed to fully see it.

He knew that no one can truly hold their life in balance, not even when in calm contemplation of it. He knew there was always a pull, sometimes amounting to an oscillation, between complacency on one side and regret on the other. He tried to favour regret, as being the less damaging.

But he certainly never regretted his love for Susan. What he did regret was that he had been too young, too ignorant, too absolutist, too confident of what he imagined love's nature and workings to be. Would it have been better—in the sense of less catastrophic—for him, for her, for them both, if they had indeed had some "French" relationship? The older woman teaching the younger man the arts of love, and then, concealing an elegant tear, passing him out into the world—the world of younger, more marriageable women? Perhaps. But neither he nor Susan had been sophisticated enough for that. He had never known sophistication of the emotional life: anyway, to him it sounded like a contradiction in terms. So he didn't regret that either.

He remembered his own early attempts to define love, back in the Village, alone in his bed. Love, he had ventured, was like the vast and sudden uncreasing of a lifelong frown. Hmm:

love as the end of a migraine. No, worse: love as Botox. His other comparison: love feeling as if the lungs of the soul had suddenly been inflated with pure oxygen. Love as barely legal drug use? Did he have any idea what he'd been talking about? Some years later, as it happened, he'd been with a group of friends when an excited junior doctor joined them, having just "liberated" a cylinder of nitrous oxide from the hospital where he worked. They were each given a balloon, which they inflated from the cylinder then held tightly by the neck. Emptying their lungs as much as they could, they put the balloon to their lips, and released into themselves the roar and lift of a sudden, rushing, eye-blinking high. But no, it hadn't reminded him at all of love.

Still, were the professionals any better? He took his little notebook from the desk drawer. He hadn't written anything new in it for a long time. At one point, frustrated by how few good definitions of love he could find, he started copying down at the back all the bad definitions. Love is this, love is that, love means this, love means that. Even quite well-known formulations said little more than, in effect: it's a soft toy, it's a puppy dog, it's a whoopee cushion. Love means never having to say you're sorry (on the contrary, it frequently means doing just precisely that). Then there were all those love lines from all those love songs, with the swooning delusions of lyricist, singer, band. Even the bittersweet ones and the cynical ones—always true to you, darling, in my fashion—struck him as the mere counterfactuals of sentimentality. Yes, it was this bad for us, buddy, but it needn't be this bad for you: such was the song's implicit promise. So you can listen with sympathetic complacency.

Here was an entry—a serious one—which he hadn't crossed out in years. He couldn't remember where it came from. He never recorded the writer or the source: he didn't want to be bullied by reputation; truth should stand by itself, clear and unsupported. This one went: "In my opinion, every love, happy or unhappy, is a real disaster once you give yourself over to it entirely." Yes, that deserved to stay. He liked the proper inclusivity of "happy or unhappy." But the key was: "Once you give yourself over to it entirely." Despite appearances, this wasn't pessimistic, nor was it bittersweet. This was a truth about love spoken by someone in the full vortex of it, and which seemed to enclose all of life's sadness. He remembered again the friend who, long ago, had told him that the secret of marriage was "to dip in and out of it." Yes, he could see that this might keep you safe. But safety had nothing to do with love.

The sadness of life. That was another conundrum he would occasionally ponder. Which was the correct—or the more correct—formulation: "Life is beautiful but sad" or "Life is sad but beautiful"? One or the other was obviously true; but he could never decide which.

Yes, love had been a complete disaster for him. And for Susan. And for Joan. And—back before his time—it might well have been so for Macleod as well.

He skimmed through a few crossed-out entries, then slid the notebook back in the drawer. Perhaps he had always been wasting his time. Perhaps love could never be captured in a definition; it could only ever be captured in a story.

Then there was the case of Eric. Of all his friends, Eric had truly been a man of good intentions, and therefore had always ascribed good intentions to others. Hence the lack of rebuke after he'd received a kicking at the fair. In his early thirties, working in a local planning department, and with a decent little house in Perivale, Eric had become involved with a younger American woman. Ashley said she loved him; a love which expressed itself as wanting to be with him all the time and never wanting to meet his friends. And Ashley wouldn't sleep with him, no, not now anyway, but certainly later. Ashley had her faith, you see, and Eric, having been religious himself in his youth, could understand and appreciate that. Ashley wasn't a member of an established church, because look at all the harm established churches had caused; Eric could see that too. Ashley said that if he loved her, and agreed with her contempt for worldly possessions, then he would surely join her in such beliefs. And so Eric, temporarily cut off from his friends, put his little house up for sale, planning to give the proceeds to some cockamamie sect in Baltimore, after which the couple would move there and be married by some cockamamie religious theorist, or shaman, or sham, whereupon Eric, in exchange for his Perivale house, would be granted squatter's rights in perpetuity in his new wife's body. Fortunately, almost at the last minute, some survival instinct asserted itself, and he had cancelled his instructions to the estate agent, whereupon Ashley vanished from his life forever.

It had been a real disaster for Eric. He had lost his belief in the good intentions of others, and with it the ability fully to give himself over to love. If only he'd been inoculated with Susan's suspicion of missionaries. But that hadn't been part of Eric's prehistory.

It was odd how the long-dead Gordon Macleod still nagged at him. More than Susan did, in truth. She was now resolved in his mind, and would remain so, even if she would also continue to cause him pain. Whereas Macleod was unresolved. So he would find himself imagining what it was like in Macleod's head during those last, mute years, goggling at the wife who had left him, at the housekeeper and nurse whose presence irritated him, at his old pal Maurice, who said, "Down the hatch, chum," then poured whisky straight from the bottle until it soaked his pyjamas.

So, there was Macleod lying on his back, day after day, knowing that this was not going to end well. Macleod was thinking back over his life. Macleod was remembering when he had first set eyes on Susan, at some dance or tea party, peopled with girls who on the whole wanted to have fun, and men who on the whole were not in respectably reserved occupations. And she was dancing with these spivs and black-marketeers— that's what his envy turned them all into. Even the honest ones were just fancy boys and fancy men. But she went for none of them. Instead she chose that twerp with the goofy grin who could really dance—about the only thing he could do—yet whose flat feet or heart flutter had kept him out of uniform. What was his bloody name? Gerald. Gerald. And then the two of them had danced while he, Gordon, looked on. Then the twerp had died of leukaemia—they'd have done better to send him up in a bomber and let him do a hand's turn before he pegged it, in Gordon's view.

Susan was of course upset—inconsolable, they said—but he, Gordon, had stepped in and declared that he was the sort of chap she could rely on, both during the war and after. She had struck him as not exactly flighty, but a bit—what? irresponsible? No, that wasn't quite right. She eluded him, and she laughed at some of the things he said—and not just the jokes, either—and such improbable, indeed impertinent reactions had made him fall smack in love with her. He told her that it didn't matter how she felt now, because he was confident that she would come to love him in time, and she had replied, "I'll do my very best." Then they'd just thrown themselves into it, as many did during the war. At the altar, he had turned to her and asked, "Where've you been all my life?" But it hadn't worked. The being together hadn't worked, the sex hadn't worked, except for successful impregnation; but otherwise, it led to no intimacy. So, their love was a disaster. But that of course was no reason not to stay married, back in those days. Because one could still be fond, couldn't one? And there were the girls. He had long craved a son, but Susan hadn't wanted any more after Martha and Clara. So that was the end of that part of their life. Separate beds to begin with; then, as she complained about his snoring, separate rooms. But one continued to be fond; if increasingly exasperated.

So he ventriloquised Gordon Macleod, in a way he could never have done while he still hated him. Was he getting anywhere nearer the truth?

He remembered another angry man: the furious driver with red, hairy ears, hooting and shouting at him on the Village's zebra crossing. And in reply he had sneered, "You'll be dead before I will." At the time he believed that the function of the old was to envy the young. So, now that his turn had come, did he envy the young? He didn't think so. Did he disapprove of them, was he shocked by them? Sometimes, but that was only fair: what they deserved, what he deserved. He had shocked his mother with the cover of *Private Eye*. Now he was himself shocked when some YouTube thread took him to a woman singing of love gone wrong: her title, and refrain, was "Bloody Mother-Fucking Asshole." He had shocked his parents with his sexual behaviour. Now he was shocked when sex was so often portrayed as mindless, heartless, thoughtless shagging. But why the surprise? Each generation assumes that it has got sex just about right; each patronises the previous generation but feels queasy about the succeeding one. This was normal.

As for the wider question of age, and mortality: no, he didn't think he felt a panic at the shutting of the doors. But maybe he hadn't yet heard their hinges creak loudly enough.

• • •

Occasionally, people would ask him, either slyly or sympathetically, why he had never married; others assumed or implied that he must have been, back there, back then. He would deploy an English reticence and an array of demurrals, so the enquiries rarely came to anything. Susan had predicted that one day he would have an act of his own, and she had been proved right. His act, which had developed without his really noticing, was that of someone who had never—not really, not truly—ever been in love.

There was nothing between a very long answer and a very short one: this was the problem. The long answer—in an abbreviated form—would involve, of course, his own prehistory. His parents, their characters and interaction; his view of other marriages; the damage he'd seen families do; his escape from his own into the Macleod household, and the brief illusion that he'd fallen into some magical world; then a second disillusionment. Once bitten, twice shy; twice bitten, forever shy. So he had come to believe that such a way of life was not for him; and had never subsequently found anyone to change his mind. Although it was true that he had proposed to Susan in the cafeteria of the Royal Festival Hall, and later to Kimberly in Nashville. This would require a parenthesis or two of explication.

The long answer was too time-consuming to

give. The short answer was too painful. It went like this. It was a question of what heartbreak is, and how exactly the heart breaks, and what is left of it afterwards.

When he remembered his parents, he often visualised them in some old television play from the black-and-white days. Sitting in high-backed armchairs on either side of an open fire. His father with a pipe in one hand, flattening a newspaper with the other; his mother with a dangerous inch of ash at the end of her cigarette, but always finding the ashtray a few seconds before it would drop onto her knitting. Then his memory would cut to her in that pink dressing gown, picking him up late at night, and flicking her lit cigarette disdainfully out onto the Macleods' driveway. And then the suppressed resentment on both sides, as they made their silent way home.

He imagined his parents discussing their only child. Did they wonder "where they had gone wrong"? Or merely "where he had gone wrong"? Or how "he'd been led astray"? He imagined his mother saying, "I could throttle that woman." He imagined his father being more philosophical and forgiving. "There was nothing wrong with The Lad, or how we brought him up. It's just that his risk profile hadn't stabilised yet. That's what David Coulthard would say." Of course, his parents had died long before Max

Verstappen's exploits at the Brazilian Grand Prix; and his father took no interest in motor sport. But perhaps he might have found some parallel form of exoneration.

And he, in turn, now felt retrospective gratitude for the very safety and dullness he had been railing against when he first met Susan. His experience of life had left him with the belief that getting through the first sixteen years or so was fundamentally a question of damage limitation. And they had helped him do that. So there was a kind of posthumous reconciliation, even if one based on a certain rewriting of his parents; more understanding, and with it, belated grief.

Damage limitation. He found himself wondering if he had always misconstrued that indelible image which had pursued him down his life: of being at an upstairs window, holding on to Susan by the wrists. Perhaps what had happened was not that he had lost strength and let her fall. Perhaps the truth was that *she* had pulled *him* out with her weight. And he had fallen too. And been grievously damaged in the process.

I went to see her before she died. This was not long ago—at least, as time goes in a life. She didn't know that anyone was there, let alone that it might be me. I sat in the chair provided. Playing through the scene beforehand, I had hoped that in some way she might recognise me, and that she would look peaceful. These hopes were as much for me as for her; I realised that.

Faces don't change much, not even in extremity. But she didn't look peaceful, even though she was asleep, or unconscious, whichever. Her forehead was pulled into a frown, and her bottom jaw pushed out a little. I knew these ways her face worked; I'd seen them many times, when she was in obstinate denial of something, denying it to herself even more than to me. She was breathing through her nose, occasionally giving a small snore. Her mouth was clamped tight. I found myself wondering if she still had the same dental plate all these decades on.

A nurse had brushed her hair, which fell straight down on both sides of her face. Almost instinctively, I reached out a hand, planning to uncover for the last time one of her elegant ears. But my hand stopped, seemingly of its own volition. I withdrew it, not knowing if my motive was concern for her privacy, or fastidiousness; fear of sentimentality, or fear of sudden pain. Probably the last.

"Susan," I said quietly.

She didn't react, except to continue with her frown, and the obstinate jut of her jaw. Well, that was fair enough. I hadn't come with, or for, any message, let alone for any forgiveness. From love's absolutism to love's absolution? No: I don't believe in the cosy narratives of life some find necessary, just as I choke on comforting words like redemption and closure. Death is the only closure I believe in; and the wound will stay open until that final shutting of the doors. As for redemption, it's far too neat, a moviemaker's bromide; and beyond that, it feels like something grand, which human beings are too imperfect to deserve, much less bestow upon themselves.

I wondered if I should kiss her goodbye. Another moviemaker's bromide. And, no doubt, in that film, she would stir slightly in response, her frown lines uncrease, and her jaw relax. And then I would indeed lift back her hair, and whisper into her delicately helixed ear a final "Goodbye, Susan." At which she would stir slightly, and offer the trace of a smile. Then, with the tears unwiped from my cheeks, I would rise slowly and leave her.

None of this happened. I looked at her profile, and thought back to some moments from my own private cinema. Susan in her green-piped tennis dress, feeding her racket into its press; Susan smiling on an empty beach; Susan crashing the gears of the Austin and laughing. But after a few minutes of this, my mind began to wander. I couldn't keep it on love and loss, on fun and grief. I found myself wondering how much petrol was left in the car, and how soon I would have to find a garage; then about how sales of cheese rolled in ash were suffering a dip; and then about what was on television that evening. I didn't feel guilty about any of this; indeed, I think I am now probably done with guilt. But the rest of my life, such as it was, and subsequently would be, was calling me back. So I stood up and looked at Susan one last time; no tear came to my eye. On my way out I stopped at reception and asked where the nearest petrol station might be. The man was very helpful.

A NOTE ABOUT THE AUTHOR

Julian Barnes is the author of twenty-two previous books, most recently *The Noise of Time*. He received the Man Booker Prize for *The Sense of an Ending*, and has also received the Somerset Maugham Award, the Geoffrey Faber Memorial Prize, the David Cohen Prize for Literature, and the E. M. Forster Award from the American Academy of Arts and Letters; the French Prix Medicis and Prix Femina; and the Austrian State Prize for European Literature. In 2017 he was awarded the Légion d'Honneur by the French government. His work has been translated into more than forty languages. He lives in London.

Books are produced in the United States using U.S.-based materials	Books are printed using a revolutionary new process called THINKtech™ that lowers energy usage by 70% and increases overall quality	Books are durable and flexible because of Smyth-sewing	Paper is sourced using environmentally responsible foresting methods and the paper is acid-free

Center Point Large Print
600 Brooks Road / PO Box 1
Thorndike, ME 04986-0001 USA

(207) 568-3717

US & Canada:
1 800 929-9108
www.centerpointlargeprint.com